"Have you made your decision?" Ryder asked, as he approached.

He reminded Emily of a mountain . . . immovable, unsympathetic and hard. *He's just a man,* she told herself, and her shoulders squared. "I'm going to tell Josh who his father was. I'll also tell him that your family has been secretly helping us through the years and that he owes you a debt of gratitude."

Ryder's gaze narrowed on her. "That's not good enough."

Emily glared at him. "What more do you want?"

"I've been doing more thinking about this situation since I left you. Josh deserves to know he has a family who wants him. So you're going to marry me and let me give the boy the Gerard name."

Dear Reader,

Blue skies, sunshine, the scent of fresh-cut grass, a walk on the shore—some summer pleasures are irresistible. And Silhouette Romance has six more to add to your list—this month's irresistible heroes who will light up your August days—or nights—with romance!

He may act like a man of steel, but this FABULOUS FATHER has a heart of gold. Years of separation had made Gavin Hunter a stranger to his son, yet he was determined to make his home with the boy. But with beautiful Norah Bennett standing in his way, could Gavin win his son's heart without losing his own? Find out in Lucy Gordon's *Instant Father*.

Our next hero can be found in Elizabeth August's own SMYTHESHIRE, MASSACHUSETTS. Ryder Gerard may have married Emily Sayer to protect her young son, but he never intended to fall in love. *A Wedding for Emily* weaves the mysterious legacy of Smytheshire with the magic of marital love.

No reader will be able to resist the rugged, enigmatic Victor Damien. In Stella Bagwell's *Hero in Disguise*, reporter Sabrina Martin sets out to discover what her sexy boss, Victor, has to hide. Sabrina always gets her story, but will she get her man?

For more wonderful heroes to spend these lazy summer days with, check out Carol Grace's *Mail-Order Male*, Joan Smith's *John Loves Sally* and exciting new author Pamela Dalton's *The Prodigal Husband*.

In the coming months, we'll be bringing you books by all your favorite authors, such as Diana Palmer, Annette Broadrick, Marie Ferrarella, Carla Cassidy and many more.

Happy reading!

Anne Canadeo
Senior Editor

A WEDDING
FOR EMILY
Elizabeth August

Silhouette
ROMANCE™
Published by Silhouette Books New York
America's Publisher of Contemporary Romance

To the acceptance of ourselves as we are...each of
us unique in our own way.

SILHOUETTE BOOKS
300 East 42nd St., New York, N.Y. 10017

A WEDDING FOR EMILY

Copyright © 1993 by Elizabeth August

All rights reserved. Except for use in any review, the reproduction
or utilization of this work in whole or in part in any form by any
electronic, mechanical or other means, now known or hereafter
invented, including xerography, photocopying and recording, or in
any information storage or retrieval system, is forbidden without
the permission of the publisher, Silhouette Books, 300 E. 42nd St.,
New York, N.Y. 10017

ISBN: 0-373-08953-8

First Silhouette Books printing August 1993

All the characters in this book have no existence outside the
imagination of the author and have no relation whatsoever to
anyone bearing the same name or names. They are not even
distantly inspired by any individual known or unknown to the
author, and all incidents are pure invention.

®: Trademark used under license and registered in the United States
Patent and Trademark Office and in other countries.

Printed in the U.S.A.

Books by Elizabeth August

Silhouette Romance

Author's Choice #554
Truck Driving Woman #590
Wild Horse Canyon #626
Something So Right #668
The Nesting Instinct #719
Joey's Father #749
Ready-Made Family #771
The Man from Natchez #790
A Small Favor #809
The Cowboy and the Chauffeur #833
Like Father, Like Son #857
The Wife He Wanted #881
*The Virgin Wife #921
*Haunted Husband #922
*Lucky Penny #945
*A Wedding for Emily #953

*Smytheshire, Massachusetts Series

ELIZABETH AUGUST

I've lived in both large cities and small towns. I confess, I loved the small towns best. Every community, large or small, has its eccentrics and its secrets. But I've always felt that in a small town these elements become more focused. They add a touch of spice or, in some cases, discord, that seems to permeate the air and give the town a personality uniquely its own. When the thought occurred to me of creating an outwardly normal, small, conservative, rural community founded on a secret known only to a few but affecting the majority—a secret that in itself could be the basis for eccentricities—I found this too interesting a concept to resist. Thus, Smytheshire and its residents began to take form in my mind.

I have to admit, I've been shocked by how alive the people of Smytheshire have become to me. I've had a lot of fun creating these books. I hope you will enjoy reading them as much as I've enjoyed writing them.

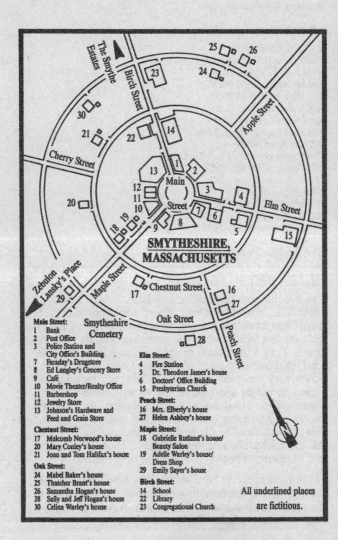

Main Street:
1 Bank
2 Post Office
3 Police Station and
  City Office's Building
7 Faraday's Drugstore
8 Ed Langley's Grocery Store
9 Café
10 Movie Theater/Realty Office
11 Barbershop
12 Jewelry Store
13 Johnson's Hardware and
   Feed and Grain Store

Chestnut Street:
17 Makomb Norwood's house
20 Mary Conley's house
21 Joan and Tom Halifax's house

Oak Street:
24 Mabel Baker's house
25 Thatcher Brant's house
26 Samantha Hogan's house
28 Sally and Jeff Hogan's house
30 Celina Warley's house

Elm Street:
4 Fire Station
5 Dr. Theodore James's house
6 Doctors' Office Building
15 Presbyterian Church

Peach Street:
16 Mrs. Elberly's house
27 Helen Ashbey's house

Maple Street:
18 Gabrielle Rutland's house/
   Beauty Salon
19 Adelle Warley's house/
   Dress Shop
29 Emily Sayer's house

Birch Street:
14 School
22 Library
23 Congregational Church

All underlined places
are fictitious.

Chapter One

Ryder Gerard stood on the front porch of his farm-house watching the first rays of sunlight come up over the horizon. The land that was now his had belonged to his great-grandfather, Zachariah Gerard. It was on the outskirts of Smytheshire, a small town, popula-tion barely fifteen hundred, located in the mountain-ous northwestern region of Massachusetts. Zachariah had been ten when his parents had moved to Smythe-shire. That had been in 1900, just one year after the founding of the town. They had thought this would be a safe place to raise their family. And for the most part, it had been, Ryder conceded.

He frowned as his gaze shifted to the barn. The loft doors were open. He remembered now that he'd for-gotten to close them last night. Impatience flickered in his dark eyes. He was in no mood to climb up there at the moment. A light breeze stirred his thick black hair.

Abruptly the wide doors swung closed. A flash of satisfaction showed in his eyes. That was one chore he could forget about.

His expression became grim as Emily Sayer's image filled his mind. She was the reason he'd forgotten the doors in the first place. He knew the time had come for him to take action. He also knew Emily wasn't going to accept his terms easily. Their confrontation yesterday at the Prescotts' had proven that.

He'd known she would be there. Thursdays were her day to clean Celina and Reid Prescotts' home. He'd purposely chosen that day to deliver the cradle he'd made for Celina's expected child. When he'd arrived at the Prescott's, Emily hadn't even attempted to appear hospitable. She hadn't been rude, just cool. She'd bluntly told him that neither Reid nor Celina was at home and suggested that he return later.

A grin tilted one corner of his mouth. The suggestion had been more like a command. The woman had spunk, he admitted, but he'd never been a man who allowed himself to be ordered around. He'd said he would wait, and he'd seated himself on the porch. He'd known before he arrived that neither of the Prescotts were home. The truth was he'd wanted to be there alone with Emily, to gauge her reaction to him. That plan had failed. She'd ignored him entirely. He, on the other hand, had been acutely aware of her moving around inside the house. But then, it seemed as if he'd always been aware of her. "Like the thorn in the rosebush you know is going to scratch you the moment you get near it," he muttered.

His frown deepened as he remembered Celina and Reid's arrival. Celina Prescott was barely through the gate when Emily came out of the house, prepared to leave. He'd meant to simply stand back and let her make her exit, but then she'd lied about why her son, Josh, hadn't mowed the Prescotts' lawn. Mentally he kicked himself. He shouldn't have mentioned seeing Josh by the river, but Emily's attempt to make excuses for the boy had grated on his nerves.

He scowled at himself. The excuses hadn't really bothered him. It was natural for a mother to be protective of her son. And he knew Josh was a good kid. It was Emily herself who'd rankled him. He had a tendency to overreact to her. She posed a threat to him and his family, and he didn't like being placed in a vulnerable position.

The sound of a vehicle brought Ryder back to the present. Looking down the long drive that led to his house, he saw his father's Jeep approaching.

Hobart Gerard parked near the foot of the steps leading up to the wide porch that spanned the front of the house. Remaining seated behind the wheel, he studied his son worriedly as Ryder descended the steps to join him.

"Morning," Ryder said as he reached the Jeep.

Hobart greeted the salutation with an impatient shrug. "You about ready to tell me what's been on your mind lately?"

"Reckon it's time for me to do my duty," Ryder replied.

"This is a touchy situation," Hobart warned. "It could cause harm to us and especially to you."

"I know," Ryder admitted curtly. "But the boy's our responsibility. I saw him down by the river yesterday. He needs a strong hand to guide him."

Hobart nodded his agreement, but his expression remained skeptical. "You've made several attempts to befriend the boy before. His mother's always stopped you."

Ryder's jaw hardened with resolve. "This time I don't intend to let her."

Emily smiled encouragingly across the breakfast table at her son. "You know you can talk to me about anything," she said coaxingly.

"There's nothing to talk about," the blond-haired sixteen-year-old replied firmly. Rising, he gave her a hug. "I've got to get going. I want to be at school early today. I promised Mr. Robinson I'd help him move some desks."

Emily said goodbye to his back as he hurried out the door. He was a handsome boy, she thought. He was already nearly six feet tall and strongly built. She wanted to attribute his physique to the fact that since he was very young he'd earned extra money doing yard work and any other kind of physical labor people would hire him to do. But grudgingly she was forced to admit it was mostly hereditary. His father hadn't been all that muscular, but his uncle was. There were other resemblances to his paternal side, too. Josh had her dark blond hair and fair complexion, but he had his father and uncle's brown eyes, high cheekbones and classic-shaped nose.

Propping her elbows on the table, she rested her head in her hands and stared down into the cup of cold coffee in front of her. Shoving thoughts of Josh's resemblance to his father's family from her mind, she concentrated on her son. Lately his behavior had seemed guarded and that had her worried. He'd always been a quiet boy but never secretive. "He's sixteen. Children go through phases," she said, hoping that saying the words aloud would convince her this was all that was happening.

She and Josh had always been so close. She'd been an unwed mother, cast out by her family. Admittedly there had been those in Smytheshire who'd helped her, but there had been others who'd looked down on her. Even before Josh was born, she'd grown to think of herself and her child as united against the world. She thought he trusted her. But in spite of his protests that nothing was wrong, she knew something was bothering him and he was refusing to talk to her about it.

"He probably thinks he's in love again," she told herself, recalling the crush he'd had on Amy Buckley. He'd come close to getting himself into serious trouble that time. Emily groaned. She still couldn't believe he'd actually stolen some of Malcomb Norwood's roses. She'd thought she'd raised him better than that. However, he had been repentant. And he'd sworn to her that he'd never give in to that kind of impulse again. Luckily Malcomb had been willing to allow Josh to do yard work to pay for the damage. She owed Samantha Brant a debt of gratitude for that.

A bitter look came into her eyes. She knew from experience that stealing a few roses was a whole lot less trouble than what he *could* get himself into. Even if it would be one-sided, she was determined to have a long talk with her son tonight. She didn't want him making a mess of his life the way she had hers. Well, not exactly a mess, she conceded. She had Josh, a roof over their heads and food on the table.

"And speaking of providing food for the table," she said, looking at her watch, "it's time for me to get moving."

But as she rose and started to straighten the kitchen before leaving for work, a knock sounded on the front door. She glanced at the clock. It was barely a quarter past seven. Wondering who would be calling on her this early in the morning, she went to answer the summons. As she opened the door, her body tensed.

"Morning," Ryder said.

He was regarding her with that same shuttered expression she was so used to seeing on his face whenever their paths crossed. She didn't blame him or any of his family for what had happened to her. She'd accepted responsibility for her actions. Still, she wasn't comfortable around any of the Gerards. Wanting to get rid of him as quickly as possible, she asked bluntly, "What do you want?"

"I've been over at my brother's grave," he replied.

Emily tensed. She'd refused to tell anyone who Josh's father was. Only she and the Gerards knew it was Hallam Gerard, Ryder's younger brother. Hiding the uneasiness Ryder's presence caused her, Emily regarded him in cool silence as she waited for him to state his business.

Resolve etched itself into Ryder's face. "I waited until Josh left. I wanted to speak to you in private," he continued, taking a step forward.

Emily took a step back to avoid colliding with him. The moment she did, she realized her mistake. She'd given him room to enter and he did. Suddenly the house seemed about the size of a matchbox. A wave of fear washed through her. "You aren't welcome in my home," she said curtly.

Ryder's gaze narrowed with purpose. "The time has come, Emily, for you and me to reach an understanding." Anger flashed in his eyes. "I want to know if you've told Josh who his father was."

Ordering herself to be calm, she straightened her shoulders and faced him levelly. "No."

Ryder scowled. "What have you told him?"

Emily was proud of having taught herself to be strong-minded and independent and not allow herself to be intimidated. But Ryder Gerard *did* intimidate her. He was a big man. He stood six foot two to her five foot five, and he weighed, she guessed, around 210 pounds to her 127. None of that weight was flab, either. Years of hard toil on his farm had made his body as sturdy as granite. But it wasn't his size as much as his bearing that unnerved her.

Furious with herself for this weakness, her shoulders straightened even more. "What is said between myself and my son is none of your business."

"It *is* my business," he corrected. "I want to know what lies you've told him."

This unfair accusation caused the hair on the back of Emily's neck to bristle. "I haven't told him any lies. I've told him I made a mistake, but don't regret having given birth to him."

"Have you passed on your family's hatred for the Gerards to him?" he asked bluntly.

Indignation flashed in her eyes. "I've tried not to pass on any of the Sayers' notions to my son. I don't want him growing up with irrational hatreds in his heart."

Ryder gave an approving nod. "I'm glad to hear that because the boy needs a man's guidance, and I've decided I'm going to be that man."

There were times when Emily had wondered if she was being unfair to Josh to keep the knowledge of who his father was from him. But trusting didn't come easy for her, and she'd been raised to be especially cautious of the Gerards. "You have no right to barge into our lives. He's doing just fine with me. We don't need anyone else."

"He came real close to getting himself arrested for vandalism and willful destruction of private property last spring over that incident with Malcomb's roses," Ryder pointed out.

She saw the glint of accusation in his eyes. Was he accusing her of not being a good mother? She glared at him defiantly. "He's made amends and he won't ever do anything like that again."

Ryder regarded her levelly. "I intend to see that he doesn't."

The implication that she wasn't capable of raising her son correctly infuriated Emily. "I don't need you to help me raise *my* son."

Ignoring her protest, Ryder continued, "I can enter his life one of two ways. The first is that I confront him. I tell him I'm his uncle and that I've tried to befriend him in the past, but you've insisted on keeping him away from his father's family. This could cause a rift between you and him. I'll admit you've done a good job raising the boy and you obviously love him. I wouldn't want to see the two of you at odds."

Emily was stunned to hear Ryder admit she'd done a good job raising her son. Still, that didn't excuse the threat in his voice or make the thought of his entering her son's life any more palatable. "I don't see why your telling him you're his uncle would cause him to turn against me. He and I have struggled through life alone. You and your family have given us nothing."

Anger caused the brown of Ryder's eyes to darken to almost ebony. "You'll recall that we tried to help and you refused. I even offered to marry you."

Emily drew a shaky breath as a rush of old memories assailed her. "I remember," she admitted. Her chin lifted. "And I told you to get out of my sight and leave me alone."

"I got out of your sight," Ryder replied dryly, "but my family has never left you on your own."

Emily's stomach knotted. Next to her own family, the last people she wanted to be beholden to were the Gerards. "What do you mean?"

"You remember that special fund Doc James used to pay for your medical expenses and to provide you with room and board at Marigold Wainwright's place?" he asked.

Emily experienced a wave of nausea. When Dr. James had told her about the special fund he had available for use at his discretion, she hadn't asked any questions. At the time, Doc had already been practicing medicine in Smytheshire for nearly a quarter of a century. He'd delivered her and all of her brothers and sisters. She trusted him. Alone and scared, she'd been grateful for the assistance. Now she had a feeling she was going to wish she'd refused the money.

"Doc said that fund had been set up by one of the town benefactors to be used for anyone he decided needed a little extra help," she said. "I assumed he was talking about the Smythes."

"The money came from my family. We concocted that story with Doc to ensure you received the care you needed."

She'd known he was going to say that, but the words still came as a blow. "I didn't accept everything Doc offered," she returned defensively. "I arranged with Marigold to work for my room and board at her place." Pride glowed in her eyes. "And once Josh was born and I got back on my feet, I tried to work out a payment schedule with Doc to pay back the money I'd accepted, but he refused to let me."

Ryder acknowledged this declaration with a nod. "I know. And, I'll admit, I admired your independence."

Emily was stunned. She'd never thought she'd ever hear a Gerard say they admired anything about her.

"But you still needed help," Ryder continued matter-of-factly. "You couldn't stay on at Marigold's once the baby was born. That was when my grandfather hit on the idea of building this house."

The color drained from Emily's face. "This house?"

"After my great-grandmother died, my great-grandfather, Zachariah Gerard, didn't want to remarry, but he was still a very virile man. He and Hilda Volney became close friends. I guess you could say they had an arrangement. She lived a ways over the border in Vermont. My grandfather, Justin Gerard, knew about her, but no one else did. On his death-bed, Zachariah made Justin promise to look after Hilda. She had a remote place on a mountain. When you got pregnant, she was seventy-five and her arthritis was making it difficult for her to get around on her own. She also had a heart condition. My grandfather hit on the idea of building a house for her here in Smytheshire and having her hire you as a live-in companion to look after her. In repayment for this house and the money we supplied Hilda, she was to keep our secret about the identity of the baby's father and to leave this house to you in her will. Since she had no close family, she readily agreed."

Emily's gaze traveled around the entrance hall of the cozy one-story, three-bedroom domicile. She'd often thought of Hilda Volney as a gift of fate. The woman hadn't always been easy to get along with. But during the eight years Emily had cared for Hilda, Emily had come to think of her as a friend. When Hilda had died, Emily had grieved deeply for her. Then Hilda's will was read and Emily discovered this house had been bequeathed to her. It had pleased her to think that Hilda had grown to think of her as a daughter. Hearing the truth behind Hilda's bequest caused a jab of hurt. "So you paid Hilda to be nice to me," she muttered, feeling foolish and betrayed.

Ryder scowled. "We didn't pay her to be nice to you. She liked you."

That he'd sensed her hurt, and made an attempt to appease her, surprised Emily. Ryder could show kindness. She knew that. She was as aware as anyone in their community that he would willingly lend a helping hand to those in need. She'd just never expected him to exhibit any honest kindness toward her.

Then Hilda was forgotten as the realization that this house had been supplied to her by the Gerards hit her full force. "I never asked for your family's help," she said, humiliated to learn she owed them so much.

His expression grew grimmer. "And you never would have accepted it if you'd known we were giving it. That's why we did it secretly. But we did provide it, and if you force me to, I'll be able to point out to Josh that we never deserted him. It was your choice to keep his lineage a secret."

Emily's mind was reeling from the discovery she hadn't survived as independently as she'd thought. And when Josh found out about this aid, she could see how her son might feel she'd been unfair to him to keep him away from the Gerards. "You said there was a second option," she said stiffly.

Ryder eyed her coolly. "This time you can do what you should have done in the first place. You can marry me. I'll adopt Josh so that he has his rightful name and will legally be a member of our family."

Emily stared at him in disbelief. She'd had no idea what he might propose as a second option, but marriage hadn't occurred to her. "Marry you?" she choked out.

"I'll give you a day to think about your choices." Ryder turned to leave, then stopped and faced her. "And don't even consider taking Josh and running away. No matter where you go, I'll find you." Having issued this warning, he strode out.

Emily stood looking through the screen door as he crossed the road to the cemetery where his old green pickup truck was parked. Even as he drove away, she continued to stand there, frozen.

Suddenly her legs felt as if they were going to buckle. Shakily she made her way into the living room and sank into a chair. She was more frightened at this moment than she'd been the day she'd told her parents of her pregnancy.

But her mother and father hadn't been the first people she'd told. Hallam Gerard had been the first. His solution was to offer her money for an abortion. Recalling the night of that confrontation, it now occurred to her that perhaps deep inside she'd realized how emotionally barren her life with her family was and that this child offered her a chance to love and be loved. All she knew for sure was that she heard herself refusing his offer. He'd been furious. It was his anger that had caused the accident that had killed him. She shivered and shook off that memory.

Then her father's face loomed in her mind. The day after Hallam's death, she determined that she had no choice but to tell her family about her pregnancy. She did, however, decide she would not reveal the name of the father. That revelation would serve no purpose other than making her own father angrier with her. He ranked the Gerards in the same category as the Devil himself.

She'd known her father would react badly to her news and she'd been prepared for one of his beatings. He was always trying to beat the evil out of his children, she recalled. As he'd hit them, he'd yell at them that he was going to beat goodness into them if he had to strip every inch of hide from their bodies to do so.

But when he'd declared her so full of evil there was no hope of salvation and cast her out with only the clothes on her back, she'd been stunned. When he'd forbidden her mother, her sister and two brothers from having anything to do with her, she'd been appalled. When they'd obeyed him without a protest, she'd been devastated.

She shivered as she recalled her first night on her own. Luckily it had been summer. She'd been too ashamed to go to anyone for help. The truth was, even if she'd wanted to seek aid, she hadn't had anyone to turn to. Her mother's parents had moved to Smytheshire soon after they were married. They'd both claimed to have no living parents or brothers and sisters. Now they were dead, and Emily's mother had been their only child.

As for her father's people, she knew they were just as intolerant of human weaknesses as their son. And she had no close friends. Actually she had *no* friends. Her father hadn't encouraged his children to develop associations with people outside the family. He'd kept Emily and her sister and brothers at home, busy with chores. Idle hands get into trouble, he'd always declared.

So she'd gone up to a cave she knew about on the Rutland farm. It was in the far northwestern corner of their property on a steep, mountainous part of the land that had been left wild. She'd found it one summer when she'd been helping Mrs. Rutland pick blackberries.

Since the age of nine, Emily had worked to earn extra money—mostly baby-sitting, housecleaning and gardening. Mrs. Rutland was one of the women who hired her regularly. In return, she had free run of their land. The cave had served as her sanctuary in the past. Sitting there through the night, she'd wondered if she

could make it her home. She could feed herself, she'd
reasoned, on the money she earned with her odd jobs.
Then the sudden fear shot through her that people
wouldn't want to continue to hire her.

She'd wanted to cry, but she hadn't. Her pride
wouldn't let her. Besides, although she was scared, she
also felt a certain sense of freedom she'd never experienced before. "At least I won't have to endure any
more beatings," she'd told herself. "And I'll find a
way to take care of myself."

The next morning she'd waited until she saw her father leave the house to check on his livestock and
crops, then she'd gone up to the kitchen door. Her
brothers and sister had already left for school; only her
mother was at home.

Clarissa Sayer had refused to allow her daughter
even to enter the house. "You've disgraced us," she
said. "Don't ever show your face around here again.
And don't go looking for help from your father's
family. Don't none of them want to be bothered by the
likes of you."

"I've come for my things," Emily replied, hiding
the hurt of her mother's condemnation behind a mask
of cold calm.

"Your father boxed them up. He's taking them into
town to give to the needy of the church," her mother
replied. "They've more right to them than you."

Emily's temper flared. "I paid for most of what I
have with money I earned," she snapped. "I'll have
my things." She stalked off the porch. The two small
boxes containing what clothing she owned were in the
back of her father's pickup. She'd taken them and left,

promising herself she would never set foot on that land again....

Emily leaned back in her chair and closed her eyes. That had been quite a day, she recalled. She'd just gotten back to the cave with her belongings when Ryder had shown up. He was eighteen at the time and had graduated from high school the past spring. All he'd ever wanted to be was a farmer. As a graduation gift, his grandfather had given him his great-grandfather's land and the house Zachariah had built. Now he lived there on his own, farming his land and tending his livestock.

"I've been looking for you," he'd said, standing in the cave opening. "I've seen you come up here before. I heard your father's disowned you, and thought this might be where you were."

Ryder's land bordered the Rutland farm on the west. But she'd never thought he'd paid enough attention to her comings and goings to know how to find her. Even at eighteen he was large and muscular. His frame seemed to fill the opening. After her experiences with her father and Hallam Gerard, she'd learned to be especially wary of men. Her hand closed around a rock as she fought down a rush of fear. If he came near her, he'd be sorry.

"You don't have to be afraid of me," Ryder said, his gaze shifting to her hand where she clutched the rock. "I'm smart enough to know better than to tangle with you."

She was surprised that he sounded as if he actually considered her a threat. Still, she continued to hold the rock. "What do you want?" she asked.

"Hallam told me about your pregnancy," he replied.

"That much I guessed. Otherwise you wouldn't be here," she returned dryly, a flush of embarrassment traveling from her neck upward.

He continued to regard her coolly. "Apparently you didn't tell your father who the father of your child is."

"I didn't see how that could serve any purpose," she replied.

Ryder gave a shrug as if to say he could see her point. "Since my brother's dead and can't fulfill his obligations, that leaves me to take care of this situation," he said in businesslike tones. "He told me you wanted money for an abortion."

She faced him squarely. "No, I don't."

His jaw tensed. "Then I guess I'll have to marry you."

This unexpected proposal stunned her. To her amazement, she even found herself considering agreeing. Then sanity returned. He clearly didn't want to marry her, and she was in enough of a mess without complicating it further by a marriage neither party really wanted. "No, you don't have to marry me. I don't want anything from you or your family," she said stiffly.

"There's no reason for you to go through this alone," he argued curtly. "My brother is as much to blame for this situation as you are."

She saw the self-righteous condemnation in his eyes. Fury filled her. "Go away and leave me alone," she ordered, pronouncing each word distinctly.

He scowled impatiently. "Really, Emily, you're being childish."

That was the last straw! "Go away," she snapped, raising the hand holding the rock as if she planned to throw it.

For a long moment, he studied her in silence. Then giving his head a shake, as if he questioned her sanity, he turned and started to leave.

"Wait!" she cried as a sudden thought occurred to her.

He turned back and silently waited for her to continue.

"Who, besides you, knows the identity of my child's father?" she asked.

"My father and grandfather," he replied.

"I want your word for yourself and for them that none of you will tell anyone. This baby is mine, and that's all anyone has to know."

Again he regarded her in tense silence. At last he said, "If that's the way you want it."

"That's the way I want it."

Again the expression that let her know he was questioning her sanity came over his face. "If you change your mind and want our help, all you have to do is ask," he said, and turned away.

When he was gone, she changed out of the dirty clothes she'd spent the night in, and went into town. She hadn't eaten since the afternoon before and was beginning to feel a little faint by the time she reached Main Street. Using some of the two dollars she had in her pocket, she bought a doughnut at the café. The moment she entered the place, she knew by the glances she received that news of her banishment had spread through Smytheshire. Stella Grayson, the elderly waitress who'd worked at the café for as long as most people in town could remember, added a glass of milk free of charge. "Guess you'll be giving up school," she said solicitously. "But you should study and get one of those equivalency diplomas. Education is important."

Her words caused Emily to realize the full impact of the change in her life. She would have to give up school and go to work full-time to support herself and her child. She thanked the woman for the milk and the advice and left.

Eating the doughnut as she walked, she went over to Doc's place. This was her usual day to go there after school and help Melba James, Doc's wife, clean. "Might as well let people know I'm going to be available during the day now," she reasoned.

But when she reached Doc's place, her situation took a turn for the better. Melba insisted that Emily stay with her and Doc until she could find suitable accommodation. The next day Doc told her about the fund that would help pay her expenses.

Emily tensed as her mind returned to the present. Even knowing that she hadn't accepted all the money offered, that she'd worked to support herself and her child, didn't help ease the shock of learning now that she'd accepted help from the Gerards.

Suddenly she needed to see Josh. She called Mrs. Elberly and told her she'd be late arriving to clean the woman's house. Then she headed to the school.

Chapter Two

"Have you come to get Josh's books?" Ruth Ann Scott, the principal's secretary asked as Emily entered the school office. "I hope he isn't very sick," she added. "I wouldn't want him missing too many more days of school this year."

Emily was already tense. Obviously Josh had skipped school today, and the implication that he'd done this several times already this year caused her to experience a wave of nausea. She felt as if her life was suddenly coming unraveled and she was powerless to stop it. "Yes, I've come for his books," she lied. Her anxiety grew as she waited for Ruth Ann to look up Josh's locker number and give her the combination.

Leaving the office, she forced herself to go and pick up his books. By the time she slid in behind the wheel of her ancient Ford, her hands were shaking. She remembered that yesterday Ryder had said he'd seen

Josh down by the river. Hoping her son had gone back to the same spot, she drove along the route she guessed Ryder had taken into town. As she crossed the bridge west of town, she saw her son. He was sitting on the trunk of a tree that had fallen into the stream and created a natural pier extending into the water. She parked on the side of the road and hiked down the embankment.

Josh had made his way off the fallen tree and to the dirt bank by the time she reached him. "Guess you're mad because I lied to you," he said defensively.

Looking up at him, she realized again how much he'd grown. Just that morning she'd been thinking of him as a boy, but he was nearly a man. "I'm more worried than mad," she replied honestly. "I wish you would tell me what's wrong. I thought we were a team."

His jaw firmed. "I've respected your wish not to talk about my father, but I need to know who he is."

She'd known this day would come, and she'd been trying to avoid it. The determined look in his eyes reminded her of his uncle. There was strong Gerard blood in her son, there was no denying it. The sudden realization that both he and Ryder had chosen this day to resolve this issue shook her. Pure coincidence, she assured herself; this situation had been building for some time. Knowing she had no choice, she said, "I'll tell you about your father, but I need to talk to someone first. I want you to go home and wait for me."

Josh frowned in protest.

Before he could launch into an argument, she added firmly, "I promise. I'll tell you what you want to know as soon as I get home."

He regarded her for a moment longer in silence, then started up the embankment.

Emily drew a shaky breath and followed. While Josh walked toward town, she climbed into her car and drove to Ryder's place. She saw him down by the barn as she parked in front of his house. By the time she'd climbed out of her car, he'd already set aside the bale of hay he was carrying and started toward her. Nervously she stood waiting for him.

As he approached, he wiped the sweat from his brow with the sleeve of his shirt. Then he removed the heavy leather work gloves he'd been wearing, slapped them on his thigh and shoved them partway into the hip pocket of his jeans. The jeans, she noted, were streaked with dust and dirt. They also fitted in a way that emphasized the sturdy columns of his legs. An unexpected surge of feminine appreciation for his male physique caused a rush of heat, and she scowled at herself. Not only was her life unraveling, so was her sanity, she groaned mentally. He was the enemy. He threatened everything she held dear.

"Have you made your decision?" he asked, coming to a halt in front of her.

He reminded her of a mountain—immovable, unsympathetic and hard. *He's just a man,* she told herself, and her shoulders squared. "I'm going to tell Josh who his father was. I'll also tell him that the Gerards have been secretly helping us through the years and that we both owe you a debt of gratitude."

Ryder's gaze narrowed on her. "That's not good enough."

Emily glared at him. "What more do you want?"

"I've been doing more thinking about this situation since I left you. You're going to do what's right by Josh. You're going to marry me and let me adopt the boy. He deserves to know he has a family who wants him."

"I'll tell him you want him," she promised.

Ryder shook his head. "He'll feel torn between you and us. The only way to avoid that is to make you a part of our family, too."

Emily's gaze raked over him. Again she was startled by the sudden heat that swept through her. He wasn't even handsome, she chided herself. But he wasn't bad-looking, either, she had to admit. He had a certain rugged charm that would appeal to women who liked the caveman type. *But, he doesn't appeal to me,* she assured herself. "I don't want to be a part of your family," she replied coolly.

He frowned. "You gave up that choice when you seduced my brother."

A rage she'd buried deep within her surfaced. "I didn't seduce your brother," she snapped. "He got me drunk and took advantage of me."

In the sudden silence that followed this outburst, Ryder's gaze became shuttered. His scrutiny unnerved Emily. Not wanting him to think she was trying to justify her own actions by placing all the guilt on his brother, she said stiffly, "I know I behaved stupidly. I shouldn't have gone out with Hallam in the first place. He had a reputation for being wild, and there were those who said he had a mean streak in him. I didn't even really like him. But he dared me to defy my father at a moment when I was ripe for rebellion. And I shouldn't have had any alcohol."

Ryder continued to watch her in silence, and she shifted uneasily. "I don't even remember much of what happened. It's all sort of like a vague nightmare. A few weeks later I became aware I was pregnant." As she realized how much she'd revealed, she flushed, and clamped her mouth shut to prevent herself from saying any more.

Ryder drew a sharp breath, and she braced herself, certain he was going to call her a liar. Instead, he said gruffly, "How Josh was conceived makes no difference now. You're going to marry me."

The anger she had kept buried so long grew more intense. "I will not be used by a man again," she seethed.

Ryder scowled impatiently. "I have no intention of using you," he assured her. "You'll have your room and I'll have mine. You will, of course, quit your outside jobs and concentrate on taking care of me and Josh and this house. I know you're used to having your own money, so I'll give you an allowance or a salary, however you wish to view it. And I'll expect you to be civil toward me so that Josh won't feel he's living in a hostile environment."

For a long moment, all Emily could do was to stare at him. Then finding her voice, she asked curtly, "What happens if I don't agree to go along with this marriage?"

"If you don't, Josh could be the one to suffer the most," he replied.

Emily knew he was probably right. Still, she wasn't ready to give up without a fight. "Either way he'll probably suffer," she said. "No doubt he'll be treated like a black sheep by your family."

Ryder regarded her coolly. "I can assure you he'll be treated as a welcome member of this family."

The truth hit her full force. "I'll be the black sheep."

Ryder made no attempt to deny this. Instead, he said, "You'll be treated with kindness."

"Tolerant kindness," she mused dryly.

Ryder frowned impatiently. "You've raised Josh well. My family appreciates that. I appreciate that."

At least he was being honest, she told herself.

"We'll have the wedding here at my place a week from tomorrow. I'll make the arrangements," he continued in a businesslike tone. "I assume you'll want to tell Josh on your own."

Before she could respond, he'd turned and started back to the barn.

"Not even a simple 'Is a week from tomorrow all right with you?' or 'What kind of wedding would you like?'" she muttered irately under her breath, still finding the reality of marriage to Ryder difficult to accept. Again she had the feeling her life was coming unraveled and she couldn't stop it. The sudden need to have the last word came over her.

"You *will* let me know what time you expect me here, won't you?" she yelled after him.

He turned and grinned wryly. "I'll be sure to let you know that," he returned, then continued on toward the barn.

Abruptly she found herself thinking that his smile had a certain rakish appeal. Stunned that this thought had even crossed her mind, she again scowled at herself. *There is nothing appealing about Ryder Gerard,* she fumed. *He's an arrogant, hardheaded bully.* She'd marry him for her son's sake, but she'd keep her distance, Emily vowed. Which shouldn't be too hard, since that was clearly how he wanted it too, she added, ignoring the piqued sensation this thought caused.

As Ryder walked toward the barn, he could feel her watching him. He'd sounded a hell of lot more confident than he felt, he admitted. This marriage could be the worse idea he'd ever had.

Emily drew a shaky breath. It was time to face her son. She slid in behind the wheel of her car and drove home.

Josh was sitting, leaning against the trunk of the big elm in their front yard waiting for her. The grim expression on his face reminded her a lot of Ryder. As she got out of the car, he rose and walked toward her.

"Let's go inside," she said.

Nodding, he preceded her to the door, then held it open for her. Her throat felt suddenly dry. She went into the kitchen and ran herself a glass of water.

"You ready to tell me his name now?" he demanded, as she finished taking a drink and set the glass aside. His voice edged with resentment, he added, "I assume it was my father you went to see to warn him you were going to tell me who he is."

She turned to face him. She was filled with fear about how he would feel toward her, but she knew she had no choice. "I went to see your uncle, Ryder Gerard. Your father was Hallam Gerard, Ryder's younger brother."

"The one who died in the car accident?" Josh asked.

Again, the mention of the crash caused a chill to run through Emily. "The accident happened a couple of days after I discovered I was pregnant," she said.

"Guess if he'd lived, he would've married you."

She heard the hopefulness in her son's voice. She'd known that not having a father had been difficult for him. But she hadn't realized it had meant so much. "Yes," she replied. She knew Hallam wouldn't have gone to the altar willingly, but considering Ryder's resolve to do what was right, she figured Ryder would have forced Hallam to marry her. That would have been a match made in hell, she thought.

"How did Ryder Gerard take the news that he's my uncle?" Josh asked, bringing her back to present concerns.

"He already knew," she told him honestly.

Surprise registered on Josh's face. "Do all the Gerards know about me?"

Emily shook her head. "No. I think only Ryder, his father and his grandfather know."

Josh scowled. "Guess they've been too ashamed of me to claim me."

Emily saw the pain in her son's eyes, and she hurt for him. The thought that maybe she'd been wrong to keep him away from the Gerards nagged at her. "No, they aren't ashamed," she said. "It was my fault the Gerards stayed away from you. I was young, and my pride was all I had left. I chose to raise you on my own and they respected my wishes. But I've recently learned that they never fully left us on our own. They've been secretly looking after us. They provided the money for my medical bills when I was pregnant with you, and they're even responsible for us having this house."

Josh raised a skeptical eyebrow as if he doubted the Gerards honestly wanted to claim him. "How did my Uncle Ryder take the news that you were going to tell me the truth?"

"He thought it was about time," she admitted. Her stomach tightened with nervousness. "He's a man who holds strong beliefs about family and duty. He wants me to marry him so he can adopt you and make you both legally and in the eyes of the community a Gerard." There, she'd said it. Marriage to Ryder! The idea still unnerved her.

Confusion spread over Josh's face. "He wants you to marry him? I thought you two didn't even like each other."

Attempting to hide her own uneasiness, Emily gave what she hoped was an indifferent shrug. "We don't know each other well enough to dislike each other. But he's offered me a reasonable arrangement, and I'm beginning to think it might be for the best."

Josh studied her worriedly. "I don't want you doing something you don't want to do just for me."

Studying him, she remembered the hopefulness in his eyes when he'd asked if his father would have married her. Being illegitimate had been more of a strain on him than she'd realized. "It's the right thing to do," she replied, parroting Ryder.

Josh didn't look convinced. "You've been good to me and I don't want you making any more sacrifices for me."

Emily hugged her son. As much as she hated the idea of marrying Ryder, a part of her knew that the man had been on target—for Josh's sake, it was the right thing to do. "It's only fair for you to be a part of your father's family," she said with conviction.

As Josh straightened away, she saw the torn look on his face. Clearly a part of him wanted to accept her decision while another part felt obligated to give her the opportunity to change her mind. Although she had serious reservations about marriage to Ryder, she was about to assure Josh that she knew what she was doing when the sound of a truck pulling up outside caught her attention.

She glanced out the window and saw Ryder approaching the house. He looked even more intimidating than usual. A wave of apprehension swept over her. Had he decided against the wedding? Had he decided to try to turn Josh against her, instead? She'd thought Ryder was the kind of man whose word she could count on, but trusting any man was stupid, she admonished herself.

Josh was already on his way to the front door. Following quickly, Emily caught up with him as he met Ryder halfway up the walk.

"Looks like your mother's told you that you're my nephew," Ryder said, studying the boy guardedly.

"Yeah," Josh replied. "She also told me that you two are talking about getting married."

"The date's set for a week from tomorrow," Ryder confirmed.

In spite of her misgivings about the proposed marriage, Emily experienced a rush of relief. At least she wouldn't have to fight Ryder for Josh and run the risk of losing her son when he learned all that had happened in the past.

Josh squared his shoulders as if prepared to do battle. "I don't want my mother being pushed into something she doesn't want."

"The marriage is to right a wrong done years ago. I'll make no demands on her," Ryder promised.

The way Josh stood up to Ryder surprised Emily. He faced the man without flinching. Ryder still had a couple of inches on Josh, and although Josh was strongly built, he was still slighter and less muscular than his uncle. Ryder also had the advantage of age and experience. He was used to being in command, and she'd seen other men cower under Ryder's scrutiny. A rush of pride flowed through her. She glanced toward Ryder and saw the glint of admiration in his eyes as he studied the boy.

"How about you coming out to my place and having lunch with me? We can have a man-to-man talk," Ryder suggested, making it clear the invitation was for Josh only.

His eyes never leaving his uncle, Josh nodded his consent. Then glancing toward his mother, he said, "I'll be back in time for dinner."

As she watched Ryder and her son walking toward Ryder's truck, the urge to run after them and insist on being taken along was strong. She'd never thought of herself as being a possessive mother. But for such a long time it had been just her and Josh standing together against the world. Now, suddenly, Josh was taking charge of his own life and she felt as if a part of her was being ripped out. "I'm not being fair. Josh needs to be his own person, lead his own life," she admonished herself under her breath. "The way he faced Ryder is proof that he's learned to stand on his own two feet. I should be proud of that.''

Still, after they'd driven away, she couldn't stop herself from pacing nervously. Ryder's image loomed large in her mind. The cool indifference in his manner when he'd assured her and then Josh that he'd make no demands on her annoyed her. She knew he wasn't attracted to her, and she didn't want him to be. But did he have to make her sound so unappealing? she fumed as she paused to take a long look at herself in the hall mirror.

Grudgingly she admitted that she looked all of her thirty-three years. Although her face was unlined, there was a tiredness in the eyes. And right at this moment, dressed for work in a pair of faded jeans and plain blue blouse, she looked stark and haggard. Her long blond hair was pulled tightly back from her face and bound by a rubber band into a ponytail. Her normally pale complexion was even paler than usual. However, her features were reasonably good and with a little makeup she could even be considered pretty, she decided. Her gaze traveled to her figure. She had curves in the right places, she saw. All in all, Ryder had no reason to find her totally unattractive.

Abruptly she scowled at herself. How Ryder viewed her was unimportant. It was silly of her even to be thinking about that. "I'm going to go stir-crazy if I stay around here," she muttered to the image in the mirror. Besides, she still had a living to earn and Mrs. Elberly was expecting her. Going into the kitchen, she made herself a sandwich. Nerves made the food taste like sawdust. After only a couple of bites, she put the sandwich in the refrigerator and hurried out.

* * *

Emily paused, lifted her arm and wiped the sweat from her brow with the sleeve of her blouse. In an attempt not to think about her son or the marriage Ryder was insisting upon, she'd been working nonstop since she'd arrived at Mrs. Elberly's house. The kitchen, the bathroom and the bedrooms were all cleaned. Only the living room was left.

"You're getting done in record time today," the elderly woman said, entering the room as Emily finished vacuuming and began to dust.

"I've been trying to make up for my late start," Emily replied.

Mrs. Elberly studied her with interest. "You're different today," she announced after a minute.

"I admit I'm more frazzled than usual," Emily conceded.

Mrs. Elberly shook her head as if this was not a satisfactory response. "Something's going on. Usually your presence doesn't interest my crystals very much."

Emily knew she was considered quite uninteresting by most people in town, and she didn't mind. She'd had her fill of being gossiped about. But to be told that even Mrs. Elberly's crystals found her boring caused a sting of insult. *You don't even really believe she hears anything from those crystals,* she said to herself, startled that the woman's words had caused her any pain at all.

"Usually when you're here they tinkle just a little. It's sort of a quiet restful sound. But today they're practically chiming," the elderly woman continued thoughtfully.

Emily glanced toward the table filled with geodes and cut crystals. Turning back toward Mrs. Elberly, she wondered how the woman would describe the crystals' reaction to the news of the wedding Ryder was planning. But the words refused to be spoken. *Because I don't really believe it's going to happen,* she admitted. *In fact, I'm having a hard time believing this day is really happening,* she added. It was like a bad dream. But this was one dream she wasn't going to wake up from.

Josh was waiting for her when she returned home. He even had a tuna-and-noodle casserole cooking in the oven.

"How was your afternoon?" she asked, trying not to show her anxiety.

"It was fine," he replied noncommittally. An uneasiness flickered over his features and he shifted uncomfortably. "You've always told me you wanted me to be honest with you."

Emily's stomach knotted with fear. Had Ryder said something that was causing her son to turn against her? "Yes," she replied levelly.

Again Josh shifted uncomfortably, then squaring his shoulders, he faced her. "Well, the truth is I'm tired of being an outsider. Not that most of the people in town haven't treated me kindly. But I've always had the feeling you and I were sort of on the outside looking in, that we've never been really accepted."

Emily choked back the lump in her throat. She'd never wanted her son to feel like an outcast. "I'm sorry. My pride was all I had left. I was determined to

make it on my own. I never meant for you to feel isolated.''

Josh put his arms around her and hugged her.
''You've been good to me and I love you.'' Then releasing her, he regarded her worriedly. ''The Gerards
have offered us a place with them. And when I was
with Ryder today, I felt as if I belonged there. He assured me again that the marriage he's proposed won't
put any demands on you, and I believe him. He's also
planning to make certain you have a secure future even
if you decide you want out of the marriage after a
while.''

Because she knew his only real concern was for
Josh, Ryder's determination to look after her irked
Emily. ''I don't need or want any charity from the
Gerards.''

Josh raked a hand agitatedly through his hair. ''I
didn't mean to imply that you did.''

Emily was angry with herself for overreacting. ''I
know,'' she said in a calmer tone. ''And I understand
how you feel.''

''Then you really don't mind going through with the
wedding?'' he asked.

Again she saw the hope in his eyes. ''No, I don't
mind.''

Relief showed on his face. ''Thanks, Mom,'' he
said, hugging her tightly.

A little later, as Emily showered before dinner, she
admitted to herself that she, too, was tired of being on
the outside. But for her there was no entry. The Gerards were only accepting her because of Josh.
''Someday I'll find a place where I'm wanted,'' she

assured herself. But for now, she'd see that Josh found his niche.

Ryder came by that evening to inform her of the procedure for getting their marriage license and to set up a time to pick her up for the blood tests.

Once these arrangements had been made, he turned his attention to Josh. "It's about time you learned to ride a horse," he said to the boy. "My dad, my grandpa and I have let a portion of our land remain wild. It's rough, heavily forested terrain. When any of our livestock gets loose and heads in that direction, it's easier to go after them on horseback. If you're interested, we can start your lessons tomorrow after school."

Josh's eyes glistened. "I'd like that."

As the boy and the man became absorbed in conversation about the care and feeding of horses, Emily realized there had been a void in Josh's life she hadn't been able to fill. And, she admitted, Ryder was probably as good a choice for a father figure as any man. To her knowledge, he was fair, honest and hardworking. The fact that he was treating her honorably was added proof that this assessment was realistic. And, watching him, she had the distinct impression he really liked her son.

On the other hand, I am a necessary nuisance Ryder feels he has to put up with. This thought left an acid taste in her mouth. Suddenly feeling the need to be alone, she decided to let the two males do their bonding on their own and she escaped to the back porch.

The wind had picked up. Swirling around her, it freed some of her thick blond hair from its loose plait and whipped the escaped strands around her face. She looked up at the night sky. Storm clouds rolled across the face of the moon. She could smell rain in the air. The night matched her turbulent mood, she thought, as she stood with an arm hooked around one of the posts supporting the porch roof.

"It's getting late. I should be on my way."

Emily jerked around to see Ryder coming out onto the porch.

"Josh is doing some schoolwork," he added, explaining the boy's absence.

"I'm glad to hear that," she replied, expecting Ryder to bid her a quick good-night and be on his way. Instead, he stood there watching her guardedly. The night seemed suddenly darker and the threat of the storm more intense. Then she realized that the weather hadn't changed; it was his presence that was causing her to be more acutely aware of everything around her. "Was there something you wanted to talk to me about?" she asked, too tense to endure his silence a moment longer.

"I've been thinking that to keep the gossip down and to make the adoption go more easily, we should let people think our marriage is a love match," he said.

Emily raised an eyebrow skeptically.

"We're both private people," he continued. "It's not out of the realm of possibility that we could have been keeping company without anyone's knowledge."

"What about our little confrontation yesterday in front of Celina and Reid Prescott?" she challenged dryly.

Ryder grinned crookedly. "They could interpret it as the remnants of a lovers' spat."

The sudden mischievousness in his eyes caught her unawares. She experienced a curious curling in the pit of her stomach, and her blood seemed to race a little faster. The realization that, at that moment, she actually found him attractive unnerved her. This whole business had her so rattled, she was having irrational reactions, she reasoned. "I suppose you're right," she said, willing to agree to anything to get him to leave more quickly.

The grin disappeared and his expression became serious once again. "I also think we should let it be known publicly that Hallam was Josh's father. His death will explain why he didn't marry you, and the fact that he was Josh's father will make Josh a full-fledged Gerard in the eyes of the town. Also, the acknowledgment of the fact that Hallam was Josh's father could make the adoption process go more smoothly. Your pride and the inbred Sayer distrust of Gerards will give the gossips a good-enough reason for your not allowing us to help with Josh's upbringing. Of course, my family will also let it be known that we didn't leave you entirely on your own. We'll also make it clear you didn't know we were providing help."

"I suppose it'll have been your perseverance and charm that won me over and convinced me you're trustworthy and worth loving," she said dryly, then found herself thinking that if Ryder ever did set his mind on courting a woman he would succeed. *But he's not interested in courting me and I'm not interested in being courted by him,* she added quickly.

"And it will have been my admiration for your ability to stand on your own two feet and weather the storm of gossip and the hardships of raising a son on your own that will have convinced me *you're* worth loving," he returned.

An unexpected wish that he did feel that way swept through Emily. *I don't want him to be in love with me—I just want him to have a few friendly thoughts toward me,* she corrected quickly. After all, they were going to be under the same roof, and life would be much easier if their relationship was amicable. "You've given this a lot of thought," she said.

"I want to undo as much of the damage my brother caused as I can," he replied.

He was again making it clear that he considered marriage to her atonement for his brother's sins. His attitude grated on her nerves. Well, she was only marrying *him* for her son's sake, she reminded herself. And his logic regarding the outward appearance of their marriage was sound. "Then consider ours a love match," she said.

He nodded with approval, then glanced toward the sky. "I want to get home before the storm hits." He was already halfway down the steps by the time he added a hasty "good-night."

A long thin streak of lightning cut through the black sky as she heard him drive away. Thunder rolled and the wind blew harder. The perfect night for a "love match" like theirs to begin, she thought wryly.

Chapter Three

The following Monday morning, Emily watched the back door swing shut as Josh left for school. Her son seemed more relaxed and happier than he had in months. As for herself, she wasn't pleased about being the center of gossip again. However, Ryder had been right concerning the town's reaction. The fact that Hallam had died before he could make an honest woman of her excused her unwed motherhood in the eyes of the majority of the residents. Besides, Josh's birth was old news. It was the announcement of her impending marriage to Ryder that was causing the most talk. She could still visualize the curious glances and the shock in the eyes of some when she'd sat in church on Sunday with Ryder and the rest of his family.

As for the Gerards, their willingness to welcome her and Josh into their fold was revealed when Ryder's grandfather, Justin, and Ryder's father, Hobart, had come by her home Saturday evening to tell her in person they approved of the marriage. Beatrice Gerard and Vanessa Norris, Ryder's sisters, had come with them. All had been openly warm toward Josh. Toward Emily they'd been kind, though guarded. But then, that was only to be expected, she reasoned.

A loud knock her front door startled her. Pushing the Gerards' visit from her mind, she glanced at the clock. It was barely seven-thirty. The only other time she'd had a caller this early, it had been Ryder. And no one else's presence could cause her more of a shock than his, she mused. The knock sounded again and she rose to answer it.

I was wrong, she thought as she opened the door and saw her father standing there. Age had added lines that gave more emphasis to his scornful, judgmental expression. And he was heavier than he'd been as a younger man, which made him appear even more formidable.

Jerome Sayer glowered at his daughter. "I waited until the boy left for school. Everyone in town is saying his daddy was Hallam Gerard and I don't like being under the same roof with a Gerard." He was clutching a pocket-size Bible to his chest like a protective shield. "I knew the Devil had you. I should have guessed it was a Gerard who had fathered your bastard."

A shiver ran through Emily. He'd always prefaced his worst beatings by clutching one of his many Bibles to his chest and making some claim about the Devil being in her and him having the duty to beat the evil out. Her back stiffened. If he tried to hit her this time, he was in for a surprise. She'd not submit so easily as she had as a child. "You're not welcome here," she said, starting to shut the door.

Moving quickly for a man so large, Jerome opened the screen door that separated them. Flattening his large hand against the wooden front door, he prevented her from closing it. "You've put your soul in grave danger by bearing a Gerard," he said, his voice carrying a warning. "There'll be no hope for you if you go through with this marriage."

"My soul is none of your concern," she retorted. "And if I were you, I'd worry about my own soul."

Jerome's expression blackened. "You'll shame your family by marrying a Gerard."

Emily used to cow under that gaze, but not now. "I have no family. You said so yourself," she replied.

Jerome trembled with rage. "The Gerards are possessed."

Emily scowled impatiently. "If you're referring to that story my great-grandfather Thaddeus Sayer told about Zachariah Gerard, it's absurd, and I'm not interested in hearing it again."

"Thaddeus swore on his mother's Bible that he saw Zachariah cause that tree to shift the course of its fall without touching it!" Jerome thundered.

"And Zachariah swore he saw the tree falling toward his daughter and he flung himself against it. To his relief, the force he was able to exert was powerful enough to shift the angle of the tree's fall just enough to miss the girl," she countered. Meeting her father's glare with an indignant frown, she continued, "And that's most certainly what happened. Because for two days afterward, Zachariah was in such pain he was forced to remain in bed. But your self-righteous grandfather nearly managed to wreck the Gerards' good reputation with his accusations that they were possessed by the Devil." Cold anger glistened in her eyes. "It seems to me the Sayers have a lust for condemning people and then enjoying watching them suffer."

Jerome straightened to his full height. "We know what's right and what's wrong."

Emily regarded him dryly. "I know about my great-grandfather Thaddeus's attempt to claim a parcel of the Gerard land as his own. And I've heard the speculation that Thaddeus's version of the tree incident was most likely an attempt to discredit Zachariah so that the court would rule against the Gerards. The ploy didn't work, but it's caused me to wonder if your judgment of what's right and what's wrong is based more on self-serving interests than on saving souls."

"You've a smart mouth, girl," Jerome bellowed, his face flushing red.

"And you're a pompous hypocrite," she snapped back, finally saying what she'd wanted to say for years.

"I'll teach you to side with Gerards," he seethed through clenched teeth.

Before Emily could move, he'd entered her house. In one smooth motion, he grabbed her with one hand as he slipped the Bible into his pocket. Then he swung at her.

She caught the full brunt of the blow on her jaw. Dazed, she would have fallen if he hadn't still been holding on to her. The old fear of his attacks swept through her. Then came rage. She kicked at his legs, but his heavy high work boots caused more pain to her toes than she did to his shins. "You've no right!" she screamed at him, attempting to jerk free.

"I'll teach you what's right!" he snarled, raising his hand to strike her again.

"Why don't you try picking on someone your own size," a male voice suddenly interrupted.

Emily looked up and saw Ryder standing behind her father. He'd caught Jerome's raised arm. No one had ever protected her from her father before. It was ironic that Ryder Gerard should be the one to come to her aid.

Jerome paled as he glanced over his shoulder and recognized Ryder. Then his expression turned to indignant rage. "Emily's my daughter. This is a family matter. Get out!"

"Being her father doesn't give you the right to beat her," Ryder said coldly, continuing to grip the man's arm. Challenge flickered in his eyes. "If you feel you have to hit someone, try me."

A sudden fear for Ryder's safety swept through Emily. Then she recalled that she'd never known her father to strike anyone he thought might be able to effectively fight back. Still, she watched anxiously as her father freed her. She would stop him if he did try to hurt Ryder, she promised herself. As she made this pledge, she was shocked by the strength of her determination to protect the brown-eyed farmer. *I just don't want him getting hurt because of me,* she reasoned.

Stepping back toward the door, Jerome jerked his arm free of Ryder's hold. Then he pushed open the screen door and stalked out onto the porch. He let the door bang closed, then glared at Emily through the thin wire barrier.

"You'll rue the day you bonded yourself to a Gerard," he snarled. And with this pronouncement, he turned and left.

Emily stood motionless, watching her father walking away. He was a cruel, vindictive man.

"You have no reason to fear me or my family," Ryder said, breaking the silence.

Emily turned to face him. "I don't. And I'll never subject myself to anyone's tyranny again. If you ever try to do me or my son any harm, I'll stop you."

A crooked smile tilted one corner of Ryder's mouth. "I'll consider myself warned."

She'd never thought Ryder Gerard could look boyishly charming, but at moment he did. Her blood seemed suddenly to warm. *Don't let yourself be fooled,* she cautioned, her hard-learned distrust bubbling to the surface. He could, in his own way, prove to be as much her enemy as his brother and her father had. Turning away, she headed down the hall. Realizing her jaw was hurting, she glanced at herself in the mirror as she passed. A bruise was beginning to show.

She was still feeling a little dizzy from her father's blow when she entered the kitchen. Sinking into a chair at the table, she leaned forward and rested her head in her hands. Aware of movement going on around her, she looked up to see Ryder dumping ice into a dish towel.

"Been in a few brawls myself," he said, carrying the cold bundle to the table. "Put this against your face. It'll help keep the swelling down."

A part of her rebelled against accepting his aid. But her practical side won out. Mumbling a gruff thank-you, she took the cold pack and, head bowed, held it against her jaw. Knowing she'd have fared much worse if he hadn't come along when he did, she forced herself to add, "And thanks for showing up when you did."

"You're welcome," he replied.

She knew he was still standing beside the table. Out of the corner of her eye, she could see the glint of his belt buckle. And a prickling on the back of her neck made her certain he was watching her.

"You hate accepting help from me, don't you?" he asked after a moment.

"Yes," she admitted, continuing to face the table and not look up at him.

He frowned impatiently. "I'd like to know why. Josh tells me you don't believe the story your great-grandfather told about my great-grandfather, so I don't understand your determination to keep him away from us."

"I have my reasons," she replied, wishing he'd just go away.

"It has something to do with my brother's death, doesn't it?" he demanded harshly. "Is it guilt?"

She turned to glare up at him. "No, it isn't guilt."

He didn't look convinced. "I've always figured you were the woman who called to report the accident but refused to identify herself. I knew he'd gone to meet you. He'd come to me for money, and I'd refused to give it to him unless he told me why he wanted it."

The bile rose in Emily's throat as ugly images flashed through her mind.

Ryder's gaze narrowed. "What happened that night? I offered to go with him when he met you, but he insisted on going alone."

The accusation in his voice caused Emily's back to stiffen. "Your brother's death was his own fault," she said curtly.

"What happened, Emily?" he asked again.

Fierce pride glittered in her eyes. "I'd agreed to meet him on that old access road that runs between my parents' place and the Rutland farm. I was waiting for him. He parked, and we talked. He offered me money for an abortion. I told him I'd decided to have the baby. He got furious and said he wouldn't marry me. I told him I wasn't asking him to. He said I didn't have to ask—you and your father would make him. I let him know he should have thought about that before he took advantage of me. He called me a few names, said I was a stupid slut." She flushed scarlet as she realized she had repeated those words aloud. "I agreed I was stupid."

Ryder made no comment.

Emily looked away. Her gaze rested unseeingly on the table in front of her as the images from that night filled her mind.

"Go on," he ordered when her pause lengthened into long seconds.

Emily drew a shaky breath. Ryder's presence was nearly forgotten as she began to relive the events that followed her argument with Hallam. "He was furious. He got into his car, started the engine and gunned it. He leaned out the window and yelled a few more obscenities at me. Then he released the brake and hit the gas. He was so angry he wasn't watching what he

was doing. He leaned out to yell at me again as he sped
away. When he did that, the car swerved toward the
deep ditch that runs along the side of the road. He
tried to jerk it back. I guess the tires on the passenger
side must have already been caught in the ditch and the
momentum threw the car off balance. Anyway, the
next thing I knew, it was flipping over. It rolled a couple of times, then hit a tree and stopped upside down.
I remember the wheels were still spinning. I ran to it.
When I looked in, I saw Hallam. There was blood all
over his face and he seemed to be staring at me with a
vacant expression. I said his name, but he didn't answer. I knew then he was dead.''

Emily paused as the memory caused a wave of nausea. Then she continued, ''The Rutland farmhouse
was closest, so I ran there. No one was home. I'd taken
care of Mrs. Rutland's cat and plants several times
while they were on vacation. I knew where the spare
key was. I got it, went inside and called the police.
Then I relocked the door and went through the woods
back to my parents' farm.''

''Hallam always did have a knack for letting his
temper get him into trouble,'' Ryder said. ''I knew I
should have insisted on going with him that night.''

The guilt in Ryder's voice surprised her. She looked
up at him. ''You can't blame yourself for what happened to your brother.''

Ryder's expression grew grimmer. ''Hallam was an
angry, frustrated man. I should have tried harder to
help him get rid of that anger.''

Emily studied Ryder. She'd considered the possibility that he would blame her for his brother's death,
but she'd never considered that he would blame him-

self for what had happened. "Has it ever occurred to you that maybe some people are just born mean?"

He scowled. "We all spoiled Hallam. I spoiled him. That makes me at least partially responsible for his behavior."

"You," she said tersely, "have an overdeveloped sense of responsibility."

Ryder shrugged off her declaration. "Who's responsible doesn't matter. It's time for me to make as much wrong into right as I can." He put his hands on the table and leaned forward, bringing him closer to her eye level. "I'm not like my brother. Neither is the rest of my family. You can trust us. We'll treat you fairly."

"Trusting doesn't come easy for me," she admitted tightly. "I've learned it's safer to keep my guard up."

His gaze burned into her. "I realize you've got good reason to feel that way. And I know you're not happy about being coerced into marrying me. But I'll take good care of both you and Josh. You can depend on me, Emily."

The thought that if she was to depend on someone Ryder would be the perfect candidate shot through her mind. "No." The word came out sharply. "That is the one thing I will never do." The words were meant as much for herself as for him. "When your brother stripped me of my dignity and my family turned against me, I made myself a promise. I vowed I would never depend on anyone but myself. I will never be stupid enough to break that vow."

Suddenly Emily couldn't face him any longer. She shifted her gaze to the table. She knew she sounded cold, but then why shouldn't she? Life had dealt her some hard blows.

Ryder studied the woman in front of him. He could understand why she'd isolated herself and her son. But that didn't make his position any easier. Their marriage, he had no doubt, was going to be difficult and certainly uncomfortable. Still, he had no choice. "I'm used to strong-willed women," he said. "My mother was one, Beatrice is another and even Vanessa has her moments. We'll find some common ground that'll allow us to live in reasonable harmony."

His hand came into her view, and she looked up to see that he'd extended it toward her.

"To compromise," he said.

"To a dubious alliance," she replied, accepting his handshake.

As Ryder's hand closed around her's, Emily was startled by the warmth of his skin. *It's a trick of my mind,* she told herself. Her other hand was holding the cold compress so that when she contacted something even moderately warm with the other, she felt the heat more intensely, she reasoned. Still, she couldn't ignore the unnerving sensation caused as the heat from his hand traveled up her arm.

Releasing her, he frowned with concern. "Let me see your face."

"I'm sure it's fine," she insisted, suddenly embarrassed both by the scene he'd witnessed between her and her father and by how disheveled she must look.

Ignoring her protest, he gently eased the hand holding the ice pack away from her jaw. "You're going to have a bruise, but I don't think you'll have a black eye."

As he touched her face, his fingers left a trail of heat on her skin. And his touch had a gentleness that made her want to lean into his hand and have him cradle her face. Shaken by her thoughts, she told herself she was still in shock from the confrontation with her father.

"Can you move your jaw?" he asked.

When he lifted his hand away from her, she felt deserted. Trying to ignore this further irrational reaction to him, she opened and closed her mouth. "It's fine," she said.

"In the future, check and see who's at the door before you open it," he ordered.

"I intend to," she replied. Forcing herself to look at him, she caught the flash of uneasiness in his eyes. Clearly he was uncomfortable just being in her company. "I know you don't really want to marry me," she said. "Surely there's another way."

Ryder shook his head. "I've given this a lot of thought. Josh could change his last name to Gerard, but that wouldn't make him a legal member of our family. I want him, both in the eyes of the law and the eyes of the community, to be a legitimate member of the Gerard clan. To do that, I need to adopt him. And, to accomplish that you would either have to give up your claim to him, which I know neither you nor he would agree to, or you and I must be married."

He hadn't denied not wanting to marry her. He had, in fact, practically admitted this was so. Pride glistened in her eyes. Determined to let him know that she felt as trapped as he did and that she had no intention of holding him to an arrangement he had no wish to maintain, she said, "Josh has told me he wants to be a Gerard, but he's also said he won't join your family without me. Besides, you're right. I can't give him up. I'll go through with this marriage for him, but I want you to know that once the adoption is completed, I intend to free myself from you."

Ryder nodded. "That would probably be for the best."

Emily congratulated herself. She'd been right; he would be glad to be rid of her. *And I'll be glad to be rid of him,* she assured herself.

Ryder's manner became strictly businesslike. "The wedding is the reason I came by. I've arranged for Reverend Carlyle to perform the ceremony at my place at eleven on Saturday morning. My sister Vanessa, her husband and their children will be there. So will Beatrice, my father and my grandfather. My father will be best man. I need to know who you'll be inviting."

Emily didn't like admitting she didn't have any close friends, but, the truth was, she didn't. Earning a living and raising her son had required the majority of her time and most of her energy.

"We might as well keep this as simple as possible," she said. "I'll have Josh give me away. Would you ask Beatrice if she'd stand up for me?"

"I'll ask. I'm sure she will." Again his gaze narrowed on her face. "I should take you to see Doc."

She was certain she heard an edge of impatience in his voice. "I don't need to see Doc, and I'm sure you have more important things to do with your day than stay here and nurse me," she said with dismissal.

For a moment Ryder considered arguing with her. Then he reminded himself that Emily Sayer could take care of herself. And she'd certainly made it clear that was how she wanted it. Which was for the best, he told himself again. Aloud he said, "I'll be by to pick up Josh after school today. He wants to learn about farming. I think the boy has a knack for it."

He couldn't get away fast enough, Emily thought dryly as the screen door closed behind him. Continuing to remain seated, she laid aside the ice pack. Her mouth formed a thoughtful pout as she pictured Beatrice Gerard. Saturday, when Beatrice and Vanessa had come with their father and grandfather to welcome her to the family, was the first time Emily had ever spoken to either of Ryder's sisters.

But Beatrice seemed like the most reasonable choice as maid of honor. She was the oldest of the two sisters, a tall slender brunette with a self-confident bearing. Emily did some quick calculations and determined that Beatrice was most likely twenty-nine. She was divorced and had taken back the Gerard name. Now she lived with her grandfather, caring for him and his house. "Besides, it doesn't matter who I choose to be my maid of honor," she muttered to herself. "This isn't a *real* marriage. It's strictly an arrangement on paper."

As if to confirm this, she heard her own words parroted back at her later that same day. She'd cleaned the Norwood house, come home and had just finished showering and changing into fresh clothes when Beatrice arrived.

"Ryder called and told me you'd asked if I would stand up for you," the pretty brunette said, as she sat at Emily's kitchen table, watching Emily pour glasses of iced tea. "I know this isn't a real marriage—the 'love, honor and cherish till death do us part' kind." She suddenly frowned as her gaze shifted to her ringless left hand. "Of course, that kind doesn't always last, either," she said. She returned her attention to Emily. "Anyway, I know you and Ryder consider this wedding simply a legal formality so that Josh can become a dyed-in-the-wool member of our family. And Ryder has told me that you're keeping the ceremony as simple as possible. But I thought I should stop by and see if there was any particular color you wanted me to wear. I don't want to clash."

"I haven't even thought about what I would wear," Emily confessed as she handed Beatrice a glass of iced tea and then seated herself.

"Then I suggest we both make a trip to Adelle Warley's place," Beatrice said, taking a quick sip of her drink as she rose from her chair. "No time like the present."

Before Emily could offer a protest, Beatrice had gently but firmly pulled her from her chair and was guiding her toward the front door.

Emily considered coming to an abrupt halt as they reached the porch, but suddenly the desire to allow herself to do something impetuous was strong. For the past sixteen years she'd lived a totally controlled life, never giving in to any frivolous impulses. *Besides, buying a new dress for my own wedding isn't exactly frivolous,* she reasoned as she climbed into Beatrice's car. Five minutes later they were parked outside Adelle's shop.

"I know you're getting ready to close, but this is a special occasion," Beatrice apologized to Adelle as she and Emily entered the dress shop housed in the lower level of Adelle's home.

"I heard that there was going to be a wedding," Adelle replied, nodding her head in approval. "And that Ryder is going to adopt Josh, too." Sympathy showed on her face. "It's a shame Hallam died before he could claim his son himself."

"We're all real proud to have Emily and Josh joining our family at last," Beatrice said firmly.

Adelle's attention swung back to Emily. Behind her smile, there was curiosity in her eyes. "I have to admit that hearing you and Ryder were getting married came as a surprise. But then, there've been quite a few matches in this town that have come as a surprise."

"My brother's been thinking about marrying Emily for quite a while," Beatrice said matter-of-factly before Emily had a chance to respond. "It just took him a while to ask her."

Emily had to admire Beatrice's finesse. The woman hadn't lied, yet at the same time she'd given credence to the rumors that Ryder and Emily had been seeing each other privately for some time.

Adelle's smile warmed further as she returned her attention to Emily. "What kind of dress do you have in mind?"

"Something summery, I suppose. And not too formal," Emily replied, then admitted, "I really haven't had much time to think about it."

Adelle shook her head disapprovingly. "A bride should have time to plan her wedding."

Emily gave what she hoped was a nonchalant shrug. "Ryder convinced me that waiting would serve no purpose."

"You know how my brother is," Beatrice added as she began going through the dresses on the rack in front of her. "Once he sets his mind to something, it's practically a done deal."

"Ryder has always been a man of action," Adelle conceded.

Emily saw the sudden flash of suspicion in Adelle's eyes and guessed that the woman was wondering if the marriage was taking place so quickly because Emily had gotten herself in the family way again. There were probably a lot of people in town wondering the same thing, Emily realized. Some were probably even laying bets on it. Well, they were in for a big disappointment.

Determined to return to the subject of dresses, she said, "I think I'd like something in pastel, maybe even a floral design."

"I've got just the thing," Adelle said, smiling brightly as she waved for them to follow her to the back of the shop.

An hour later Emily and Beatrice left Adelle's with their purchases. Emily had bought a tailored, pale pink linen suit with tiny blue and white flowers on the skirt and the lapels of the jacket. She'd also purchased a pair of white heels and a purse to go with the suit. The outfit cost more than she'd ever spent on herself before. But she wanted to look nice for the wedding for Josh's sake, she reasoned. Besides, dressed in the suit, she looked like a woman in control of her world. Admittedly she felt as if she was standing in quicksand, but she wasn't about to let anyone else know that.

"I can't believe how lucky we were. The blue of the dress I found is almost a perfect match for the flowers in your suit," Beatrice said as they drove back to Emily's.

"At least we'll be properly dressed for our parts in this production of Ryder's," Emily replied, fighting back a surge of what felt like panic.

Pulling up in front of Emily's house, Beatrice set the car in Park and turned to her. "You and my brother are doing the right thing," she said with conviction. "Josh should have been brought into the family a long time ago."

Emily had the feeling that Beatrice wasn't as positive about this marriage as she was trying to sound. "I promise you, I won't cause Ryder any grief," she assured the brunette. "I'll release him from this union as soon as the adoption is completed."

Smiling encouragingly, Beatrice reached over and gave Emily's hand a squeeze. "Everything will work out for the best. I know it will."

Despite Beatrice's attempt to hide it, Emily saw the shadow of doubt in the woman's eyes. Forcing a return smile, she gathered up her packages, thanked Beatrice for helping her shop for the dress and went inside.

She couldn't blame the Gerards for not trusting her. After all, there hadn't been any kind feelings between the Sayers and the Gerards for three generations. Still it hurt to know that they would have preferred to claim Josh without having to include her.

"Well, I'm not asking to be one of them," she murmured. But again she found herself thinking that it would be nice to feel wanted.

Chapter Four

Emily stood in the center of Ryder's living room, flanked by Gerards. Ryder was to her right, his father beside him. Beatrice was to her left. Josh was behind Beatrice. Next to him was Justin Gerard, Ryder's grandfather. He was an older version of Ryder and Hobart, with a thick head of white hair, clean shaven, and skin weatherworn and permanently tanned from a lifetime of working outdoors. Beside Justin was Les Norris, Vanessa's husband, Vanessa and their two children. Reverend Carlyle was in front of her giving his usual short sermon on the sanctity of marriage before completing the vows. The Reverend was near seventy now and had served as pastor of the Presbyterian Church in Smytheshire for nearly forty-five years. He'd baptized both Emily and Ryder and watched them grow up.

Emily wasn't certain the old minister had bought their story about a secret courtship. She was certain he was worried about the marriage's survival. But he hadn't tried to talk her and Ryder out of going through with it. When they'd gone in for the required chat with him, she had the impression he thought they were doing the right thing for Josh's sake. However, he was putting a bit more vigor than usual into his sermon.

As for the Gerards, they were obviously determined to make this appear to be a festive occasion. Ryder had simply told her to show up a little before eleven on Saturday morning, and she had. She'd been stunned to discover the living room of his farmhouse decorated with balloons, streamers and flowers. And there had been a bridal bouquet for her, corsages for his sisters and boutonnieres for the men, including Josh. On a table in the corner was a wedding cake topped by the traditional toy wedding couple.

Emily had to admit that Ryder had created the perfect setting for a wedding. Or maybe Beatrice had, she amended, recalling how Beatrice had taken her in hand and helped her pick out a suitable outfit for the occasion. And Emily was glad she'd splurged and bought something nice. She still *felt* like the unwanted weed in the rose garden, but at least she *looked* as if she belonged.

Her mind snapped back to Reverend Carlyle. He was asking her to repeat what he was saying. She obeyed. Then Beatrice handed her the ring. Ryder had said that the members of his family had always had double-ring ceremonies. To maintain the air of authenticity he wanted for their wedding, he'd purchased the man's ring that matched the plain band she'd chosen.

Taking Ryder's hand in hers, Emily thought she'd never touched a hand that felt so strong. A current of electricity seemed to travel up her arm. *I'm simply overreacting because of nerves,* she told herself. As she slipped the ring on his finger, a tremor of apprehension shook her. She'd been so certain she could face this marriage with stoic resolve. But at the moment her legs felt like jelly. Releasing Ryder's hand, she breathed in deeply, attempting to calm the panic threatening to take hold of her.

You're behaving like a silly child, she admonished herself as Ryder began to repeat his vows. *This is a simple arrangement for Josh's sake. I'll be a live-in housekeeper, that's all. Ryder will most likely completely ignore me.* As proof of this, she recalled that he'd spent as little time in her company during the past week as possible.

Her body suddenly tensed. Ryder had taken her hand in his and a current of electricity again shot through her arm. She looked down as he slipped the ring on her finger. A sense of being protected and secure enveloped her, and suddenly she *felt* as if she belonged there. Startled, she raised her gaze to his face. His expression was serious, almost grim. *He looks like a man doing his duty,* she thought, and the feeling of belonging vanished. She wasn't wanted here.

"I now pronounce you husband and wife. You may kiss the bride," Reverend Carlyle intoned.

Emily knew that for the Reverend's benefit, Ryder was going to kiss her. But the look in his eyes made her believe he'd rather be kissing one of his cows. Well, she had as little desire to kiss him as he had to kiss her.

As his face moved toward hers, she felt herself bracing for the contact. *I'll probably feel like I'm being kissed by a fish,* she told herself in an effort to ease the nervousness that threatened to overwhelm her. All week she'd tried not to think about this moment. When she had, the thought had brought on a case of the jitters. Ryder Gerard was a virile-looking man, and she'd been living almost a cloistered life since the night his brother had taken advantage of her. She'd dated a little, but had never felt any interest in even kissing the men she'd gone out with. She'd finally decided that the incident with Hallam had left her frigid.

Ryder's arms circled her loosely. She was acutely aware of his strength. His body heat warmed her. She drew a steadying breath and caught a whiff of his after-shave. It was mildly spicy she noted, experiencing an unexpected rush of pleasure. Then his mouth found hers. The contact was light and dispassionate. But as he lifted his head away, she could still feel the imprint of the kiss like a brand burned into her lips. Her heart was pounding violently and her legs were weak. *I'm just very nervous,* she told herself. And she had a right to be. She'd just married a man who didn't want to marry her and to whom she didn't want to be married. Her body stiffened and she forced a smile for the Reverend.

"Congratulations." Hobart Gerard broke the silence that had fallen over the proceedings.

The next thing Emily knew, she was being hugged by him and then by the rest of the family. It occurred to her that she would have enjoyed this show of acceptance if it had been for real. But when she looked beyond the smiles of the adults and into their eyes, she saw anxiety and concern. Vanessa's two children, Larry, who had just turned four, and Gwyne, who was two, were standoffish.

"They're shy around people they don't know," Vanessa said apologetically when she tried to get them to hug their new aunt and both clung to their mother, instead.

"That's natural," Emily replied, her own smile beginning to feel plastic. She guessed the children had overheard their parents voicing worries about this marriage, or maybe they simply sensed their parents uncertainty.

For Reverend Carlyle's benefit, she squatted down to eye level with the children and said, "I'm sure we'll be great friends soon." What surprised her was how much she wanted that to happen. *Don't go wishing for the impossible,* she warned herself.

"I hate to leave before you serve the food," the minister said. "But I've got another wedding to perform today." He turned to Emily. "Mrs. Gerard, would you walk me to the door?"

The use of her new name shook her. *It's only a name and it's only on loan,* she reminded herself. Even though she was surrounded by people, she felt alone. Glad of the excuse to escape for a few moments, she smiled and hooked her arm through the Reverend's.

He said his goodbyes to Ryder and the rest of the family in the house. But when he and Emily reached the door, he kept her at his side, forcing her to accompany him on out to his car.

He was elderly and getting forgetful and a little hard of hearing, but she knew he didn't miss much. She guessed he'd noticed the tension. Clearly, he wanted to speak to her alone.

At the door of his car, he gave her hand a fatherly pat, and met her gaze. "Hallam Gerard was a bad seed. He had a mean streak in him. But Ryder is a good man. There's no one in this town I trust more. He'll be a good husband to you and a good father to Josh." He smiled encouragingly. "The rest of his family are good people, too. Beatrice can be a bit blunt, but at least you'll always know what she's thinking. In time, they'll all come to accept you as one of them." He gave her hand another pat. "It's about time you found a place for yourself. I never liked your being so alone."

She was still alone but she wasn't going to tell the Reverend that. Instead, she smiled and said, "I know Ryder is a good man, and his family are good people."

"Good luck to you, girl." He gave her hand another pat, then released her. "You deserve it."

Emily had grave doubts about good luck ever finding its way to her door, but she was grateful for his kind words. "Thank you," she replied, then started back toward the house.

As she mounted the short flight of steps to the porch, she saw Ryder standing in the doorway. He came out of the house and waved goodbye to the elderly clergyman as he drove away. Then Ryder turned his attention to Emily.

"I suppose Reverend Carlyle had some last-minute advice for you," he said, his intonation making this more of a question than a statement.

"He told me you were a good man." An edge of challenge entered her voice as she added, "One I could trust."

"You can trust me," he assured her.

Again it occurred to Emily that if she was to trust someone completely, Ryder Gerard would be a good candidate. She still wasn't about to let her guard down though.

Ryder motioned toward the door. "We should be going inside. Beatrice and Vanessa were cooking all morning. They've laid out a regular feast."

Emily's nerves suddenly snapped. "I would have helped with the decorations and the cooking. Brides aren't usually simply told to show up just before the ceremony. They normally have something to do with the planning and preparations. I feel like a guest everyone felt obliged to invite but didn't really want to have around."

An expression of apology spread over his face. "I guess my family isn't real sure how to act about our marriage. We all need to sort of adjust to one another. My sisters and I were just trying to make this day as easy as possible for you."

A flush of embarrassment reddened Emily's cheeks. Even though this wedding was his idea, it was clearly as difficult for him as it was for her. "It's my turn to apologize," she said. "You're right, this arrangement is going to take a lot of adjusting to on all sides."

He looked relieved. "For Josh's sake, we can make it work."

Emily thought of how much happier her son had been since he'd discovered the Gerards wanted him. For the first couple of days he'd watched her closely, obviously concerned about her feelings. But she'd put on a cheerful front and finally he'd relaxed.

"Yes, for Josh's sake, we will make this arrangement work," she replied.

"Are you two coming in? Everyone's getting hungry," a youthful male voice suddenly asked from the doorway.

Emily looked past Ryder and saw Josh. There was a worried look in his eyes as if he was afraid there was already trouble between his mother and uncle. She forced a smile. "Yes, we're coming in. I'm famished, and Ryder tells me Beatrice and Vanessa have prepared a terrific spread."

Josh grinned in relief. "They must've been cooking all week," he said. Then turning to Ryder, he looked mildly self-conscious. "I was wondering what I should call you now—Dad or Uncle Ryder?"

"How about just Ryder?" Ryder suggested.

Emily saw the genuine smile on Ryder's face. Obviously not only was Ryder accepting Josh as a full-fledged member of the Gerard clan, he honestly seemed to care for her son. For that she was grateful. Josh deserved to have others in his life he could lean on besides her. Her gaze traveled to Ryder's broad shoulders. Ryder certainly looked like someone who'd make a good leaning post, she thought, unexpectedly picturing herself leaning against that sturdy shoulder. The image brought a rush of warmth.

"You ready to go back inside?"

She looked up into her new husband's face. The smile was still there, but the expression in his eyes was guarded. The warmth she'd experienced a moment earlier turned to a chill. Ryder wouldn't have given her the time of day if Josh hadn't been his nephew. And she didn't need him or anyone to lean on, she told herself firmly.

"Yes," she replied with calm resolve. Then turning to Josh, she added with forced enthusiasm, "Lead the way to the food."

A couple of hours later, Emily found herself sitting at the kitchen table watching the two sisters wash dishes. She'd volunteered to help, but they'd insisted she shouldn't have to work on her wedding day. So Emily had relegated herself to taking care of two-year-old Gwyne. The little girl's initial standoffishness seemed to be wearing off.

Which was more than Emily could say for the rest of the Gerards. Beneath their polite surface friendliness, she still sensed underlying doubt and uncertainty about her. Following the ceremony, when they'd all sat down to eat, she'd been aware that in their own way, each family member was struggling to find some common ground with her.

To her relief, after only a brief spurt of exchanges welcoming her into the family, the men had turned their attention to the crops, livestock and weather.

That left only the sisters and Vanessa's children for Emily to deal with. Attempting to ease the underlying tension in the atmosphere of the table, she'd talked to Vanessa about her children and to Beatrice about quilting. Beatrice was considered one of the finest quilters for miles around and sold her work to tourists and locals alike. But even when she was talking about her craft, Emily noticed the woman did not entirely relax.

Finally, feeling she'd done her best to put the sisters at ease, Emily had concentrated on making friends with Vanessa's two children.

Now the eating was over, the men, including Josh and Vanessa's young son, Larry, were in the living room and the women were in the kitchen cleaning up.

"You have a real way with children," Vanessa said to Emily as she dried a pot and smiled at her daughter, who was now crawling onto Emily's lap. "Gwyne doesn't take to just anyone these days. She's at that stage where she's shy around anyone who isn't family." She suddenly flushed. "Of course you're family now. I just meant that she probably doesn't really know that yet, so that makes it unusual for her to be so good with you."

"I understood what you meant," Emily said, attempting to placate the woman's obvious embarrassment.

"Understanding Vanessa's reasoning would try the sharpest mind," Beatrice interjected.

Emily saw the older sister toss Vanessa a reproving glance. She also thought she saw a warning there.

Vanessa's lips tightened as if holding in whatever she'd been planning to say next. Watching Vanessa as she returned her attention to the pan she was drying, Emily had the distinct impression that the sudden absence of conversation in the room was making the woman decidedly uncomfortable. She tried to think of something to say, but she'd never been good at small talk and her own uneasiness was making it difficult for her to choose a subject for idle chatter.

Like a cork popping out of a bottle, Vanessa broke the silence. "I can't believe Ryder is actually married," she said, the words tumbling out one on top of the other. "I'd just about given up on him. I'd started thinking that he wasn't ever going to let a woman tie him down." Her mouth formed a thoughtful pout as she put the pot away. "Of course, I guess you couldn't really say he's tied himself down. This isn't exactly a traditional marriage."

As this last statement hung in the air, Vanessa spun around to face Emily, embarrassment again causing her to flush. "Of course, we don't expect him to go out chasing other women," she added quickly.

Beatrice frowned apologetically as she, too, turned toward Emily. "My sister is the kind who talks when she's nervous. Generally she puts one foot in her mouth and then the other. It's best to ignore her at times like this." Turning to Vanessa, she said with command, "I'd suggest you concentrate on drying the pots and pans and forget about making conversation."

Vanessa tossed her sister a haughty glance, then returned her attention to Emily. "I don't normally say the wrong thing all the time," she said defensively. "But I do seem to be having trouble saying the right things today."

Emily was actually grateful to the woman. "I realize this situation is difficult for all of you," she replied, grabbing this opportunity to be open about her relationship with Ryder. "And I can understand your being uncertain about how to treat this marriage. Why don't you just think of me as a temporary, live-in housekeeper for Ryder?''

Vanessa smiled with relief. "I can handle that," she said, and turned her attention back to the dishes.

Emily saw Beatrice shake her head at her sister as if she found Vanessa's behavior unbelievable. Then drying her hands on her apron, she approached Emily. "My sister means well. You'll get used to her after a while." She extended her hand. "Welcome to the family."

The sincerity in Beatrice's voice startled Emily. She felt as if she'd just passed some sort of test. "Thank you," she replied, accepting the handshake. "And I don't mind Vanessa's straightforwardness. I prefer openness and honesty."

"Yes, under most circumstances, that's best," Beatrice said.

Emily was surprised by the qualifier, and she caught a flash of uneasy glances between the sisters. But that didn't make any sense, she thought. Beatrice had a reputation for being bluntly honest—so blunt many people thought she was almost brittle. As for Vanessa, she seemed totally open.

Appearing to turn her full attention back to Gwyne, Emily covertly studied the sisters. They'd returned to doing the dishes and the tension in the kitchen seemed to have diminished some. *I'm just overreacting,* she decided.

I'm so tired my legs feel weak, Emily thought as she stood on Ryder's porch waving goodbye to the last of their guests. It was midafternoon. The Gerard clan had stayed long enough to be polite, but she had the feeling they were relieved to be on their way. Except maybe for Gwyne, she amended. Her new niece seemed to have taken quite a shine to her. But now Gwyne, as well as everyone else, was headed home.

Josh was standing on one side of Emily. Ryder was on the other. Catching a glimpse of the dark-haired farmer out of the corner of her eye, she conceded that maybe nerves had a little to do with the shakiness she was feeling along with her exhaustion. This was to be her first night under Ryder's roof.

"I need to check on the stock," he said, breaking the silence that had descended over the porch as the last car disappeared from view. He turned to Josh. "You want to come with me?"

"Sure," Josh agreed quickly.

During dinner Emily had heard Ryder telling his family how well Josh worked with the animals. Earlier in the week, Josh had been telling her about helping Ryder in the fields. Her son's eyes had glistened, and she'd realized then that, like his uncle, he seemed to be a natural-born farmer.

Ryder grinned with approval at the boy's enthusiasm, then gave Josh's tie a playful tug. "We better change first."

Emily's gaze traveled over the two males. They were both dressed in suits and, she admitted, they made a handsome pair. The thought that Ryder looked especially good flashed through her mind. She scowled at herself. Ryder's appearance was of no concern to her!

As Josh hurried inside, Ryder said "I like that suit you chose to wear, Emily."

Startled by the compliment, Emily's guard suddenly came up. If he thought he could renege on his

part of their agreement and claim his husbandly pre-
rogative, he was going to have a fight on his hands.
But his gaze was cool. He was merely making a polite
comment, she realized. He'd probably only said it because he thought it was required. She chided herself
for thinking he was the least bit interested in seducing
her. He'd made it clear from the start that was the last
thing he had on his mind.

"Thanks," she replied levelly. Then in the same
impersonal tones he'd used with her, she added, "You
looked very nice today, too."

For a moment he regarded her in silence, then he
frowned. "It'll take some doing, but we'll get used to
having each other around," he said, then turned and
went into the house.

Emily had the impression this last statement was
made as much for himself as it was for her. Clearly he
was as uncomfortable as she was. *Think live-in
housekeeper and you'll make it through this just fine,*
she ordered herself as she, too, went inside.

Going up to her room, she changed into a pair of
jeans and a shirt, then began unpacking the boxes of
personal items she'd brought over the day before. She
was kneeling beside a box of books when a knock
sounded on the door. "Come in," she called out, as-
suming it was Josh. But as the door opened, she
caught a glimpse of a pair of worn cowboy boots she
knew didn't belong to her son. Her gaze traveled up
sturdy male legs clothed in faded jeans. A heat per-
meated her body. Quickly she shifted her gaze to Ryder's face and rose.

"I was just wondering if there was anything left at
your place you wanted Josh and me to pick up for you

before we go check on the stock," he said, his expression shuttered.

"No, I think I've got everything I need for now," she replied. But even if she'd forgotten something, she wouldn't feel comfortable asking Ryder to get it for her, she admitted. He was Josh's friend, not hers.

Ryder took a step back out of the room, then stopped. "I was also wondering what you're going to do about your house and the rest of your stuff—furniture and such. People will find it peculiar if you simply let it sit idle."

Emily had been doing a lot of thinking about that house since she'd discovered the true story behind it. She knew it would never feel like her home again. "I thought I'd rent the place furnished for now," she replied. Her back stiffened. "And it's Josh's house. I'm going to have the title changed to his name and have the rent money put into an account under his name."

Ryder scowled. "I know how much you hate accepting anything from me and my family, but that house is yours."

"Then it'll be my gift to my son," she replied.

Ryder shook his head at her stubbornness, then left.

Emily knew she was being hardheaded, but her pride was all she really had in this world—that and Josh. But her son had his own life to lead, and she'd promised herself long ago that she wouldn't cling to him. Going over to the window, she looked out and saw the man and boy heading for the barns. They were talking and laughing. A sense of acute loneliness swept over her. "I'm just tired. It's been a long day," she murmured and returned to unpacking her things.

A little later, when she left her room, she glanced at the door across the hall. Ryder's room. The designation loomed like a neon sign in her mind.

The house was a large, two-story structure. There were four bedrooms and two bathrooms on the second floor. Emily remembered having heard that Ryder had remodeled the place a few years ago. Originally there had been five bedrooms and one bathroom, but he'd had the smallest bedroom converted into a second bathroom so that the master bedroom had a private bath.

Just looking at the closed door of his room caused a current of nervousness. She was glad she wouldn't be sharing a bathroom with the man.

Her gaze shifted down the corridor. The smallest of the three remaining bedrooms was on Ryder's side of the hall. It was the guest room. The other bathroom was next to her room, and Josh's bedroom was just beyond. A hint of a smile played at one corner of her mouth. She'd already begun to think of the second floor of the house as being divided into Ryder's side and her side.

"And as long he stays on his side and I stay on mine, we'll get along just fine," she muttered.

She frowned abruptly, stunned that the possibility that she could ever be tempted to cross the hall had even entered her mind. Of course she would stay on her side of the hall. Admittedly, Ryder had a certain rugged appeal, but...

She issued a frustrated growl, furious she'd even made this assessment of the man. "Well, he doesn't appeal to me," she declared.

The thought that she'd devoted too much time to raising her son and too little time to her own life crossed her mind. She shrugged it off. She hadn't chosen to have a close relationship with a man simply because she hadn't found anyone who interested her. "And Ryder doesn't interest me either," she stated firmly. Her mind, she reasoned, was just following a few crazy trails because she was tense and exhausted.

Determined to put the farmer out of her mind, she continued down the hall to Josh's room and looked in. He'd been bringing his things over all week. They were unpacked and put away. In fact, the room looked just as it had in their old home except he had more space here.

She shook her head at the sight of his suit lying on his bed. He was normally good about hanging his clothes up, but then today wasn't what she'd consider normal. Feeling a need to be useful, she entered the room and hung up the suit for him.

As she went back out into the corridor, her gaze once again crossed to Ryder's side. She wondered if he'd hung up his suit. He didn't seem like the untidy sort. Certainly his home was spotless. Of course, that could have been Beatrice's doing. She knew his sister had been cleaning for him on a weekly basis. Of course, now Emily would be taking over the maintenance of the house. "So I might as well know the worst," she said, marching across the hall.

The door of his bedroom was partly opened. She pushed it wider. There were no clothes strewn around the room. Clearly, he'd hung up his suit. Her attention moved to the large four-poster bed. It was made. Of course Beatrice could have come up and straightened the room today, she reasoned. Tomorrow Emily would begin to learn Ryder's real habits.

"Are you looking for anything in particular?"

Emily spun around. Ryder was standing behind her with an expression of displeasure on his face, as if he found her survey of his room an invasion of his privacy. Her back stiffened with defiance.

"As the new housekeeper, I was merely making a quick inspection to see if there was any tidying that needed to be done," she replied.

"I generally take care of myself pretty well," he said.

She had the feeling she was being told to get out of his room and stay out. Well, if that was the way he wanted it, then that was fine with her. She met his gaze coolly. "If you want to do your own dusting, vacuuming and laundry, that's fine with me."

An expression of uneasiness played across his face. "Nope, I don't want to do that," he admitted. "The house is your domain. Consider yourself free to roam where you will."

"Thanks," she replied tersely, feeling even more unwelcome than ever.

Ryder raked a hand agitatedly through his hair. "Look, I'm sorry," he apologized. "I don't mean to sound inhospitable. It's just going to take me a while to get used to having you here."

She glared at him. "I don't like being here any more than you like having me here."

"I know," he replied, looking angry with himself.

"Mom? Ryder? Is something wrong?" a youthful worried voice asked.

Glancing around Ryder, Emily saw Josh coming up the stairs. "No, nothing," she replied with a forced smile. "I was just asking Ryder when he thought you two would want supper."

"I'm still stuffed from the wedding feast," Josh replied, looking amazed that she could even think about food.

"The reason I came in was to tell you I was going to take Josh riding," Ryder said in an easy drawl, his tone relaxed as if he and Emily had been having a perfectly friendly conversation. He turned and grinned with approval at the boy. "He seems to be a natural horseman."

Josh beamed. His gaze swung to his mother. The smile on his face dimmed. "Mom should learn to ride, too," he said anxiously.

Emily knew her son well. It was obvious he was worried that she might feel excluded. *But I'd rather feel excluded than like an intruder,* she thought. "I think I'll just stay here and rest," she said.

Josh looked at Ryder, his expression a plea for help. Ryder's gaze leveled on Emily. "I've got a third horse and saddle. This day has been difficult on all of us. Some fresh air and exercise would probably do you good."

Clearly Ryder was only making this request for her son's sake. Pride demanded that she refuse.

Before she could respond, Josh interjected encouragingly, "It'll be fun doing something all together— just like a family."

Emily saw the hope in the boy's eyes and knew he was wishing they *could* be a real family. But that was never going to happen. However, she was beginning to feel that the walls of this house were closing in on her, and the invitation of fresh air and exercise sounded too good to resist. To pacify her pride, she told herself that she would simply ignore Ryder's presence.

"Sure, why not?" she replied.

Chapter Five

"Don't you need to give Mom some instruction?" Josh asked as he saddled his and Ryder's horses.

Ryder had just returned with the gray mare from the east pasture for Emily.

"Your mom knows how to ride," Ryder replied, tossing a blanket and then a saddle onto the horse's back.

Surprise registered on Josh's face. "She does?" He turned toward Emily. "You never told me that."

Some of the better memories of her childhood flashed through Emily's mind. "It's been a long time," she said.

Ryder's gaze was shuttered as he, too, turned toward Emily. "She used to ride bareback on her father's horse. She'd get him up to one hell of a fast pace. I thought she was going to try to make him jump a fence once."

Emily stared at him. She'd thought she'd been totally alone those days when she sneaked out to the back pasture to ride. Her father didn't believe in anyone having fun. He'd kept a horse to use for transportation when he wanted to hunt up in the mountains or inspect the portions of Sayer land that couldn't be reached by Jeep. But his children were not allowed to ride the beast for anything so frivolous as fun. He'd have given her a good switching if he'd ever learned what she'd done.

"My mom did that?" Josh asked, clearly amazed she'd ever shown any inclination for adventurous behavior.

"Yeah," Ryder replied. "It's a wonder she didn't break her neck." He frowned as he recalled the headaches watching Emily had caused him. While she'd stopped short of the fence, there was a small gully toward the west side of that pasture she'd jumped. The horse landed heavily and nearly threw her. After that, she'd given up jumping. But that horse hadn't been the most graceful animal in the world. It could stumble just walking across that field. Emily, Ryder mused, had always been a threat to his peace of mind.

Emily caught the flash of disapproval Ryder cast her way as he turned his attention back to saddling the mare. Her back stiffened with defiance. He had no right to judge her. She'd done the horse no harm, and those few moments of freedom had been precious to her.

Josh missed seeing Ryder's reproving glance. He was too busy studying his mother. "You never talk about your childhood," he said thoughtfully.

"There isn't much to tell," she replied. At least nothing she wanted to talk about, she added to herself.

"Time to mount up," Ryder announced, breaking the sudden uncomfortable silence that had fallen over the group.

As Emily moved toward her mount she noticed that Ryder had remained where he was.

"Thought I'd give you a leg up," he said as she reached the animal. His gaze was again shuttered as he added, "Her name's Lady Gray and I'd prefer if you took it easy on her."

The control Emily had been exercising on her nerves all day snapped. "If you're so worried about my harming your animal, then I'll just stay here." Turning sharply, she started back toward the house. A hand with a grip like iron closed around her arm. She jerked around and found herself looking into Ryder's dark eyes.

"I'm not worried about the horse. I just don't want you breaking your neck on our wedding day," he said.

She was acutely aware of him. An intense heat radiated from his touch. His breath teased her skin. He smelled of hay, sweat and horses, and she found herself thinking that this odor was more exciting than any expensive after-shave.

"Mom?" Josh's concerned voice broke into her consciousness.

Her gaze swung to her son. He was watching her and Ryder anxiously. Her control returned. She shifted her gaze back to Ryder. "I guess I'm just a little tense today," she said.

"We're all a little tense today," Ryder replied.

She expected him to release her. Instead his hold on her arm remained. A command for him to let go formed in her mind, but died in her throat. The brown of his eyes had darkened, and she saw desire flicker in their dark depths. She licked her suddenly dry lips. She wanted him to kiss her. *You're crazy!* her inner voice accused.

Abruptly his gaze became shuttered and a coldness descended over his features. Releasing her, he took a step back. "Shall we get mounted?"

"Yes," she said, managing to keep a sharp edge out of her voice. As she strode past him, she added firmly, "I'm sure I can get into the saddle on my own." Her outward calm masked an inner fury. Clearly he was attracted to her, but was displeased with himself for this emotion. Obviously he considered her unworthy of him. *Egotist!* she seethed.

Ryder kept his distance as she mounted. Good thing he did, she thought as he swung into the saddle and took the lead. Her fury had built until she thought she might have actually slapped him if he'd touched her again.

She drew a deep breath of the mild June air and tried to concentrate on the landscape. But the passion she'd seen in Ryder's eyes taunted her. Her mind traveled back to earlier in the week—to the day her brother had called on her.

Patrick Sayer looked like his father, from his muscular stocky build to his facial features. He was six years younger than Emily, and as children she'd always mothered him. When he'd turned against her as quickly as the rest of the family, the hurt had been doubled because she'd thought of him as her one ally.

His defection, more than anything, had caused her to promise herself she would never again seek support from anyone.

But old hopes never die, she thought dryly. Four days ago when she heard a car pull up in front of her house and looked out to see Patrick climbing out of the vehicle, the wish that he'd come to bid her well had filled her. But the grim judgmental expression on his face—an expression almost identical to the one her father always wore—vanquished that wish.

"I thought you should be warned," he'd said when she opened the door.

"You could at least show some politeness—say hello and ask how I am before you begin to lecture," she admonished. A mask of cool indifference hid the sharp hurt caused by the memories of his rejection. It was an old hurt, one she'd thought she'd put to rest, but she'd been mistaken. Having him there brought back the pain.

Remembering her own manners, she stepped to one side. "Won't you come in?" she invited.

He scowled with distaste as he stepped over her threshold. "I debated about coming at all, but I remembered how you used to watch over me. I've always felt I owed you a debt for that. This is my way of repaying it."

He made it sound as if he considered her kin to the Devil and his debt to her a sword hanging over his head. "We owe each other nothing," she said.

Ignoring this declaration, he continued coldly, "I thought you should be made aware that Ryder has a mistress. She lives near Plainfield. She's a widow, several years older than him, in her mid- to late forties. Never had any children. Ryder's been visiting her for years. Guess he doesn't want to marry her because she's barren.'' His gaze became colder. ''The only reasons he's marrying you are that he has proof you're capable of bearing children and the Gerards want your son. 'Course the boy is half Gerard, anyway. They might as well have him.''

Emily had bristled at her brother's self-righteous tone and the implication that Josh was somehow tainted. ''My son is a good, decent human being. That's more than I can say for you and your hypocritical condemnations,'' she'd snapped. ''Get out of my house!''

''Gladly,'' he'd replied, relief to be escaping her company evident on his face.

Pushing her brother out of her mind, Emily found her gaze shifting to the back of Ryder's head. She hadn't been surprised to discover he had a mistress. She'd told herself the thought of his visiting the woman while he and Emily were married wouldn't bother her. After all, he was a man and their marriage was to be in name only. But right now her stomach was tightening into a knot. *Ryder Gerard's personal life is none of my business,* she told herself firmly.

''Ryder and his dad have dredged out several deep holes and stocked the stream that runs through their property, so the fishing is real good,'' Josh said, his voice breaking into her thoughts.

She looked to her left and saw that her son had slowed his horse enough to fall into pace beside her. She'd been so intent on Ryder, she hadn't noticed when Josh had begun talking to her. Now she tried to catch up with his conversation. He was pointing ahead of them, and she could hear the sound of fast-moving water.

"The stream starts on Great-grandpa Justin's farm. Ryder says it's spring fed. It runs through Grandpa Hobart's land and Ryder's, then into the Green River," Josh continued.

She read the silent plea in his eyes. He wanted her to like it here as much as he did. The sound of the water was very close now. Coming out of the thick woods, she found herself at a creek about ten feet wide. The crystal-clear water looked to be only a few inches deep. Watercress grew thick along both banks.

"We can cross here," Ryder said, urging his horse into the water.

"Isn't it terrific?" Josh asked, his tone encouraging her to agree.

"Very," she conceded.

He smiled broadly. "Mom likes your place," he informed Ryder.

Ryder glanced over his shoulder at Emily and raised an eyebrow skeptically.

"The scenery is pretty," she said noncommittally.

He nodded in agreement. But as he turned away, she noted that he hadn't smiled or offered the slightest encouragement for her to enjoy herself. *Obviously he doesn't want me to like his place so much I might want to stay,* she thought dryly. If Josh hadn't been present, she'd have been tempted to add that this was a nice place to visit but she wasn't interested in living here. However, for her son's sake, she remained silent.

"Ryder has promised to teach me how to fly-fish. I'm sure he'll teach you, too. Won't you, Ryder?" Josh asked, clearly determined to persist in his quest to make his mother feel welcome in his uncle's world.

Again Ryder looked over his shoulder at Emily. "Sure," he said with an easy smile.

Josh grinned in relief, a look of triumph on his face.

But Emily had noticed that Ryder's smile hadn't reached his eyes. She'd be about as welcome on a fishing expedition as a fox in a henhouse, she thought making up her mind to find convenient excuses in the future so that Ryder wouldn't have her company forced on him.

Emily groaned in frustration. Through her window she could see that it was still late at night. Lifting her head, she looked at the clock on the bedside table. It read one-fourteen. When she, Josh and Ryder had gotten back from their ride, they'd had a quick supper of leftovers. Then she'd pleaded exhaustion and gone up to her room.

Ryder and Josh had gone out on the front porch to sit and talk. Her bedroom windows faced the front of the house and their voices had floated in. They'd been discussing horses during supper, but now they were talking about Ryder teaching Josh woodworking. It was common knowledge in Smytheshire that during the winter Ryder kept busy making furniture. He'd built a barn just to house his equipment. And Emily had to admit he did very nice work. The cradle he'd given Celina Prescott as a gift for her baby had been beautifully crafted. Emily was also aware that several of the townsfolk had purchased pieces from Ryder, and she was sure he'd made many of the pieces of furniture in this house.

Attempting to ignore the males below, she'd let her gaze travel around the room. It was filled with her things, but she still felt like an intruder. The sound of Ryder's voice drifting in didn't help. She considered closing the windows, but that would rob her of a pleasant breeze. Her back muscles threatened to knot. Deciding that a hot shower might help, she took one. The heat had a soothing effect on her taut muscles, and by the time she was finished, she felt more relaxed.

But as she left the bathroom to return to her own room, she nearly collided with Ryder. She was wearing only a terrycloth robe. The way his eyes raked over her, she had the impression he was seeing through to her nakedness. Then an anger flashed in his eyes as if he considered her conduct in bad taste.

"Sorry," he apologized, stepping aside to allow her to pass.

Without a word, she'd gone on to her room. But as she'd entered and closed the door, she'd had a strong urge to pack her things and leave. If he hadn't had his own bathroom and dirty clothes hamper, she'd have been tempted to return to the bathroom and collect her underthings from the hamper in there so he wouldn't have to see them.

"Our adjusting to each other isn't going to be difficult," she muttered to herself as she dried her hair. "It's going to be impossible."

She'd gone to bed as soon as her hair was dry, but she hadn't fallen asleep immediately. Instead, she'd lain there trying to relax but finding herself listening to the sounds around the house. The shower in her and Josh's bathroom was running and she assumed her son was in there. To give credence to this assumption, when that water was switched off, she heard water running from across the hall in the vicinity of Ryder's private bathroom.

She'd closed her eyes, hoping for sleep but, instead, found herself creating a mental picture of how Ryder would look unclothed. A heat stirred within her. This unexpected train of thought shocked her, and she quickly vanquished the image from her mind. For the next hour she tossed and turned and finally drifted off into a restless slumber.

Now she was awake again! Even worse, she had a vicious headache.

Tossing off the covers, she left the bed. Her aspirin was in the medicine chest in the bathroom, but when she went to take a couple, she discovered there was no glass.

Swallowing back a groan, she quietly carried the bottle downstairs to the kitchen. "Get a glass," she ordered herself in a hushed voice, her head pounding so hard she was having a hard time focusing her thoughts. Setting the aspirin aside, she opened a cabinet and took out a glass. She filled it with water, then set it aside and picked up the bottle of aspirin. Cursing under her breath at the safety lid, she finally managed to get the bottle open and jostled out two tablets.

"Are you all right?"

Emily jerked around at the sound of Ryder's voice. The movement caused an extra-sharp jab of pain in her head. Startled by both him and the pain, she accidentally knocked her elbow against the glass of water. It started to teeter. Her gaze shifted to the counter. She gasped at the unwelcome sight of the glass threatening to fall and spill, and another sharp pain shot through her head.

The water sloshed back and forth, then to her relief the glass righted itself leaving only a small spill.

"Are you sick?"

She looked up to see Ryder standing directly beside her. He was dressed only in a pair of jeans. His hair was mussed as if he'd just gotten out of bed. But there was an alertness about him that caused her to think he hadn't just awoken. "I have a headache," she said. Turning away from him, she concentrated on taking the aspirin. When she turned back, she noticed he'd moved several feet away. "Headaches aren't contagious," she grumbled.

"You looked a little too dangerous to get too near," he replied.

Pride ordered her to meet his gaze. She expected to see ridicule in his eyes. Instead, there was desire in their dark depths. In spite of her throbbing head, a shiver of excitement raced through her.

Abruptly his gaze became shuttered, and for the second time in less than twenty-four hours, she felt the brunt of his rejection. Defiance flashed in her eyes. She hadn't invited his attention!

"I'll turn off the lights," he said, stepping aside to give her plenty of room to pass.

"Thanks," she replied with an indifferent shrug. But although she managed to show no reaction to him on the surface, beneath she was acutely aware of him as he followed at a discreet distance.

"The man's impossible," she seethed under her breath as she climbed back in bed. Then she scowled at herself. Why was she even reacting to him? He meant nothing to her. Still, the vision of him watching her with passion-darkened eyes haunted her as she drifted off to sleep.

"I look like something the cat dragged in," she mused the next morning as she finished brushing her teeth and took a long look at herself in the mirror. And here it was Sunday, and she'd be expected to appear in church beside Ryder and Josh and the rest of the Gerard clan.

Making certain her robe was securely belted, she went down to the kitchen. A percolator with freshly brewed coffee was sitting on the counter.

"Ryder will be in in a few minutes," Josh said, coming through the back door as she poured herself a cup. "We've been taking care of chores. I came in to make sure you were up so you'd have time to dress and have some breakfast." A hopeful note entered his voice. "I told Ryder you make terrific pancakes."

Emily stopped herself from saying that even if she wanted to, which she didn't, she doubted her cooking would win Ryder's heart. Josh was old enough and mature enough to know she and Ryder would never be a real couple. She didn't need to keep telling him that.

"If it's pancakes you want, it's pancakes you'll get," she said. "Now run upstairs and get cleaned up."

Josh smiled brightly and obeyed.

In spite of her determined disinterest, as Emily began gathering the ingredients she needed, she found herself wondering about the winning of Ryder's heart.

From girlish chatter in high school and tidbits of gossip through the years, she knew there'd been those who tried. But to date, as far as she knew, no woman had even come close. Of course, there was the mistress her brother had mentioned. But if Ryder was in love with the woman, why hadn't he married her? Emily suddenly froze in midmotion. Surely he hadn't been waiting around all these years, putting his life on hold, just so he could marry her and make Josh a Gerard! And if he and this woman he spent time with were in love, how did she feel about this marriage? "Ryder's heart and Ryder's personal life are none of my business," she told herself curtly, forcing her full attention on mixing the pancake batter.

"Morning."

Emily had been concentrating so hard on measuring and pouring ingredients she hadn't heard Ryder's footsteps on the back porch. His gruff tones startled her and she spun around. Her hand hit the side of the bowl holding the almost completed batter, sending it sliding toward the edge of the table. Her reflexes too slow to grab it before catastrophe struck, she gasped, certain it was going to fly off and crash to the floor. But instead, it slowed and came to a halt at the very edge of the table. *At least I've got a little luck left,* she thought, grateful she hadn't caused a mess.

"You've got to stop being so jumpy around me. I'm not going to bite you."

Ryder's harsh words cut through her panic. Turning to face him, she saw him regarding her with an impatient scowl.

"Mom's always a little jittery in the morning before she finishes her first cup of coffee."

Emily's gaze shifted to the doorway that led into the hall and saw Josh standing there. He was making excuses for her behavior, trying to smooth over the rough patches between her and Ryder. A wave of sympathy for him swept through her. He was in for a big disappointment if he honestly thought there was a chance she and Ryder could ever be a real couple. But she couldn't bring herself to hurt him unnecessarily. Besides, she didn't like Ryder thinking he had such a powerful effect on her that every time he entered a room she almost spilled something. "Josh is right. I usually don't really wake up before my second cup of coffee," she lied.

"I'll keep that in mind," Ryder replied, his expression relaxing. Striding toward the door through which Josh had just entered, he added, "I'll go get cleaned up before breakfast."

To Emily's relief, she had no more near accidents as she finished preparing the meal, and the pancakes turned out perfectly. As he finished his second stack, Ryder even complimented her.

Josh's face lit up. "Mom's a great cook!" he proclaimed enthusiastically.

Ryder smiled indulgently, and Emily guessed Josh had been attempting his matchmaking on the farmer, also. But it wasn't working. Even when Ryder paid her the compliment, there had been a certain standoffishness in his eyes. Now he quickly turned the conversation to his livestock. *He'd rather discuss cows than me,* she thought wryly. Well, she'd *rather* he discussed cows than her, she affirmed, as she forked another bite of pancake into her mouth.

A little later she wished she'd stuck to coffee and skipped solid food entirely. Her breakfast was sitting like a lump in her stomach. When she, Josh and Ryder had arrived at church, most of the congregation greeted them with words and smiles of congratulations. Then she saw her parents and brothers and sister and their families gathered near the old oak on the front lawn watching with disapproval. Actually it was more than mere disapproval. It was condemnation.

When Jerome, Jr., her older brother, started toward her, the pancakes had suddenly felt like lead pellets. He looked ready to start a fight. Then she'd seen him stiffen and stop. She glanced to her side. Ryder was there watching her brother with a warning look in his eyes. Turning back, she saw fear on Jerome's face. This was quickly followed by a sneer of self-righteousness. With a shrug to suggest he considered any confrontation with Ryder beneath his dignity, Jerome turned and walked back to the family circle.

Emily breathed a sigh of relief. Turning to Josh and Ryder, she saw that the rest of the Gerard clan had joined them, forming a formidable guard. *Apparently my brothers, like my father, don't like to go up against odds that are equal or better than theirs,* she mused. It had been a long time since she'd even thought of the Sayers as family, but at that moment she was embarrassed to have ever been one of them.

"I'm sorry," she said quietly, her gaze traveling over those gathered around her.

"No need to apologize," Ryder replied.

"A person can't choose their family," Beatrice added.

Josh took her hand and gave it a little tug. Following his lead, she moved toward the church. Ryder fell in on her other side and the rest of the Gerards followed. But even with their united show of support, Emily remained uncomfortable as she sat through the service.

Through the years, she'd grown used to her family's shunning her. She'd even gone back to church and been proud of herself for being able to ignore their presence. But today their dislike felt almost tangible, and she continued to be embarrassed for Ryder and his family as well as for Josh. By the time the service was over and she, Ryder and Josh were on their way back to Ryder's place, the muscles in her neck were threatening to knot.

She'd left a pot roast cooking slowly in the oven while they were gone. As soon as they reached the farm, she put dinner on the table.

"Josh, you need to study this afternoon. I remember you telling me you have a book report due for English class tomorrow," she said as they sat down to eat. "And I'm going to go back to our place and finish packing the things I want to keep with me." She was grateful that Josh had brought everything of his to Ryder's place during the past week. She needed some time alone.

"I'm sure Ryder will be happy to help you," Josh volunteered the man quickly.

Mentally, Emily shook her head. Her son wasn't going to miss a single chance to play matchmaker. She just hoped he wouldn't be too disappointed when the adoption was completed and the marriage ended.

"Yeah, just let me know if you need any help," Ryder said.

"I'm sure I can handle this on my own," she replied with equal politeness.

Ryder nodded and returned his attention to his food. Emily saw the disappointment on Josh's face. She was going to have to have a firm talk with her son, she decided.

When the meal was over, Ryder insisted that he and Josh would clean up the dishes. Emily started to protest, then called herself an idiot. She was nearly desperate to escape and have some time to herself. Why in the world should she argue with Ryder's offer?

"Have fun," she said with a smile and hurried up to her room to change.

She heard them in the kitchen as she came back downstairs a few minutes later. Sticking her head in the door, she saw Ryder scrubbing pots and pans while Josh dried. "I'm leaving," she said.

"Call if you need any help," Josh instructed.

"Yeah," Ryder added over his shoulder.

Emily noted that although Ryder's response was polite, it lacked enthusiasm. He had to be tired of Josh's matchmaking, she thought. And it was up to her to put an end to it.

"Josh, could I speak to you alone for a moment?" she said in a tone that was more of an order than a request. She saw the hesitation in his face and knew he'd probably guessed what she was going to say and didn't want to hear it. "Josh," she repeated his name with even firmer command.

"Be right back," he said to Ryder. Then with the expression of someone facing the inevitable, he walked toward her.

Emily led the way to the front porch. Deciding they were far enough away from the kitchen not to be overheard, she turned to her son. "Ryder and I entered into this marriage so that you could have your birthright," she said levelly. "But you can't expect any more than that."

He issued a resigned sigh, then frowned impatiently. "I'd like for the two of you to at least be friends. You could try for that, couldn't you?"

Emily had known it was important to Josh for her to feel welcome in the Gerard clan. But until this moment she hadn't realized just *how* important. "Ryder and I will have to find our own common ground," she said. She had grave doubts that Ryder would ever honestly want to list her among his friends, and she refused to make a promise she wasn't certain she could keep.

Josh's frown deepened. "But you will try to find some common ground, won't you?" he persisted. "I know you're used to standing on your own, and you taught me to do the same, but living that way can get downright lonely at times."

Emily's back stiffened. He was talking as if she was in total control, as if she could make Ryder be her friend. "Finding common ground is a two-way street," she replied tersely. "Ryder will have to do some searching, too."

Josh looked contrite. "I know. I just want all of us to be happy together."

I'd settle for just feeling halfway comfortable together, Emily thought. Aloud she said, "Ryder and I will learn to get along just fine. Don't worry about it." Her expression became stern. "And stop pushing for more."

Reluctantly Josh nodded his agreement.

Emily gave her son a hug, then headed to her car. But a little later as she parked beside the house that had been her home for so many years, the feeling of having arrived at a sanctuary was missing. The knowledge that the Gerards had provided this roof over her head made it seem more their house than hers.

"It's Josh's," she told herself, and he'd want her to feel welcome here. With this thought firmly in mind, she went inside.

Tomorrow, she'd put an ad in the local paper to let people know the place was for rent, and she'd see a lawyer about putting the title in Josh's name. Going from room to room, she made a final inventory of what she wanted to take with her, what she wanted to store in the attic and what she wanted to leave out for tenants to use.

As she finished loading the last box in her car, she glanced over her shoulder at the cemetery. Without even really thinking about what she was doing, she closed the trunk of the car, then turned and walked across the street. She moved along the gravel road that wove among the graves till she came to the Gerard family plot. Silently she read the names on the tombstones until she came to Hallam's grave. There she stopped and stood staring at the ground.

"I came by to see if you needed any help."

Emily jerked around and saw Ryder standing only a few feet away. "I didn't hear you approaching," she said, her voice holding a hint of accusation.

"That's probably because you were concentrating so hard on hating my brother for what he did to you," Ryder replied grimly. His shifted uncomfortably. "And I can't blame you for feeling that way."

"I do hate him," she admitted. "But on the other hand, I love Josh and I'm glad I have him in my life."

Ryder continued to regard her darkly. "Do you come here often to glare at my brother's grave and curse him?"

Emily scowled at the farmer. He made her sound vindictive. "This is the first time I've sought out his grave," she said. "And I wasn't thinking about him as much as I was thinking about myself."

Ryder raised an eyebrow quizzically.

The unspoken question in his expression urged her on. "I was wondering how different my life would have been if I hadn't gone out with your brother that night. I was wondering if I'd have become a self-righteous bigot like the other members of my family."

Abruptly she clamped her mouth shut. She wasn't used to confiding her innermost thoughts to others, and she couldn't believe she'd revealed these particular ones to Ryder Gerard.

"Probably not," he said.

Surprise registered on Emily's face. "You actually sound like you mean that."

"You were always fighting your father's reins. That plow horse was proof of that. So was Hallam." For a moment guilt again shadowed his eyes, then they became shuttered. "When it became necessary, you faced your family, and when they judged you harshly, you didn't crumble or beg them to forgive you. You walked away from them and made a life for yourself."

The hint of a smile played at one corner of his mouth. "I'd always thought of you as a strong-willed female, and you proved me right." His expression again became solemn. "And you've got a good heart. You've proved that in the way you've raised Josh."

"Thanks," she managed, finding it difficult to believe how much his opinion of her mattered. *It shouldn't matter at all,* she told herself, but it did, and right now she was nearly glowing inside.

"Speaking of Josh," Ryder continued. "I was hoping we could tell him you and I have found some common ground, declared a full-fledged truce and agreed to be friends. Maybe then he'll relax and let us have some peace so we can adjust to each other."

Embarrassment replaced the inner glow. "Obviously Josh had a talk with you after he and I talked."

Ryder nodded. "I know the boy wants more than we can give. But he'll settle for a comfortable friendship. I realize it's going to take us a while to get to that point, but I figure life will be easier for all of us if we try a little harder to reach it."

Emily called herself a fool for letting his opinion of her matter. Clearly, even though he didn't think the worst of her, he didn't have any great confidence in the two of them ever being real friends, either. But he was trying to find a compromise, and her sense of fairness insisted she cooperate. "We both have Josh's best interests at heart," she said. "That should be common-enough ground for us to begin with."

Ryder looked relieved. "Here's to common ground," he said, offering her his hand.

Emily accepted it. To her chagrin, as his hand closed around hers, she felt as if a warm protective glove had wrapped itself around her hand, and a heat traveled up her arm. The memory of how he'd looked shirtless—his broad shoulders and hard flat abdomen enticingly provocative—was suddenly vivid in her mind.

Don't be an idiot! she admonished herself. Her gaze shifted down to Hallam's grave. She'd paid dearly for the lesson one Gerard had taught her. She needed no lessons from another.

Chapter Six

Emily lay staring at the ceiling of her bedroom, her expression one of self-directed fury.

The first week she and Ryder had been married, she'd had to leave his home each day because she still had people who depended on her to clean their houses. By the second week, most of her clients had found someone else. Now it was the third week of her marriage, and she had only Ryder's house to tend to.

She'd been telling herself from the first day of this marriage that the strong reactions she was having to him were due merely to the stress of adjusting to her new situation. She'd assured herself that with time, she'd be able to easily ignore the man. But that hadn't proved to be the case. Instead, her awareness of him seemed to have increased. She told herself she was keeping track of his whereabouts because by knowing where he was she could avoid any more contact than was absolutely necessary. But that didn't explain the dreams she'd been having. Lately they'd been about Ryder and had become more and more erotic.

In these nightly illusions, he'd pursue her, then back off. She'd flirt with him, inviting him to kiss her, but just before their lips would actually meet, he'd suddenly pull away and turn his attention to some shadowy female in the background.

This morning had been the worst yet. Emily had awoken feeling drained and frustrated. "They're just dreams," she seethed under her breath as she abruptly tossed off her covers and rose. "They've got nothing to do with reality. He's a good-looking virile man. Obviously the lusty female side of me I thought I didn't have was merely lying dormant. It's awakened, and Ryder is in my dreams because I'm living under his roof. When I see him at breakfast, I'll laugh at myself for ever allowing my fantasies to focus around him."

But a little later she wasn't laughing. It wasn't fair that he looked so appealingly masculine, she thought as she stood at the stove cooking eggs. She was keeping her back toward him, trying to block his image from her mind. But as she turned to the table with the plate of eggs, she couldn't stop her gaze from traveling over him.

The grim set of his jaw should have been a turnoff, but it wasn't. Instead, she wanted to run her finger playfully along it to see if she could make him smile. Then there were his shoulders. The urge to stand behind him and gently massage them just so she could feel their strength beneath her palms was close to overwhelming. She was having fantasies about the man in broad daylight, she wailed silently. Quickly she shoved the plate of eggs in front of him, then returned to the stove to begin Josh's breakfast.

A little later as she stood at the kitchen sink washing the dishes, a movement beyond the window caught her eye. Even before she looked up, she knew Ryder was out there. And she was right. He and Josh were on their way to the barns. She ordered herself to return her attention to her dishes but, instead, her gaze lingered on Ryder's hips. They had an easy swing to them, she thought. Her gaze shifted to his legs. His jeans fit snug around the sturdy thighs. A heat surged through her as she imagined how it would feel to have her body pressed close to his. A sudden panic threatened to overwhelm her. *I've got to get these fantasies under control.*

What she needed was something to keep her both mentally and physically busy, she decided. His attic suddenly came into her mind. She'd been up there a couple of days ago to put a box away for storage. The place was a mess—boxes, furniture, trunks, framed pictures and a variety of other discarded objects haphazardly filled the space. Dust and cobwebs were everywhere. Her expression brightened. That was the solution! She'd clean Ryder's house from top to bottom, beginning with the attic.

A little later, armed with a variety of cleaning materials, Emily climbed the narrow staircase at the end of the upstairs hall. Pushing the trap door above her open, she climbed into the storage area.

"This room could take a week all by itself," she murmured, as she stood surveying her surroundings. The attic was one huge open space with a ceiling a

good eight feet high along its center and sloping gently downward on both sides. Sheets of heavy plywood
had been nailed down to provide sturdy flooring. A
window at each end of the long room plus a naked
lightbulb located in the center of the ceiling rafters
gave her light.

Breathing a sigh of relief to have so much to occupy her time, she set to work.

Emily stood staring down at the framed canvas. It
was a large painting, around four feet by three feet.
She'd found it wrapped in a sheet and tucked away in
one of the dark corners of the attic. When she'd removed the covering so she could shake the dust out,
the painting had captured her imagination. It was a
scene of a heavily wooded area. There was an old man
with long white hair and an equally long white beard.
He was dressed in a long brown loose-fitting garment
that reminded her of a monk's robe. At his side was a
boy of about ten, wearing a sort of tunic. He was
holding a plant and it appeared that the old man was
lecturing him.

Emily couldn't resist carrying the painting to the
nearest window for a better look. The colors were deep
and rich and caused a glow of pleasure within her. The
characters portrayed brought a smile. The stern look
on the old man's face contrasted with the mischief in
the boy's slightly crooked grin. She had the feeling
that the old man had his hands full with that particular youth.

"What are you doing up here?"

Startled by the unexpected intrusion, Emily jumped
slightly, then scowled as she turned to discover Ryder

climbing into the attic to join her. "I wish you'd quit sneaking up on me," she said curtly.

He frowned at her accusation. "I wasn't sneaking up on you." His gaze shifted to the painting and then back to her. "What are you doing up here?" he asked again.

His manner was polite, but there was an edge in his voice that made her feel like a trespasser. "I came up here to clean," she replied. "I figured I'd give your house a thorough going over starting from the top." Her shoulders straightened. "However, if there are areas where I'm not welcome, I wish you'd simply tell me and I'll stay out of them."

An expression of self-directed impatience came over Ryder's features. "You're welcome to go wherever you wish in this house." His gaze shifted to the painting. "What do you think of it?"

His tone was casual, she noted, but she had a feeling the question had not been idly asked. "I like it," she replied. "There's a hint of humor in it that makes me smile."

"My great-uncle Norman painted it."

Emily glanced at the artist's signature. There was no name, only the initials N.G. in flowing script. "Your grandfather Justin's brother?" she questioned. Since early childhood she'd been made aware of the Gerards' lineage, so she knew that Justin Gerard, Ryder's grandfather, had an older brother. This brother hadn't taken to farming. He'd preferred numbers in a ledger to digging in the dirt.

"I thought he'd become an accountant and lives in Boston," she said.

"He was and he did," Ryder replied. "But he retired several years ago. His wife had died a few years earlier. He bought a fairly large plot of land in New Hampshire and built himself a home in the middle of it. He lives pretty much like a hermit—hunting, fishing and painting."

Emily's gaze returned to the canvas. "He's very talented."

"That painting used to hang in the room you now occupy," Ryder continued in an easy drawl. "I figured you might not like it, so I had Beatrice pick out something else."

"No offense, but I'd prefer this to that print of a bouquet of flowers." Emily mentally gasped at her honesty. "The flowers are nice," she said quickly. "But this painting sort of catches my fancy." Forcing her attention away from the picture, she turned to Ryder to discover him studying her narrowly.

As if making an abrupt decision, he moved forward and picked up the painting. "Then you should have it," he said.

Watching him descend the ladder, Emily drew a shaky breath. Clearly he was trying his hardest to make her feel at home here. But she doubted she would ever be comfortable under his roof.

Today she was feeling her most uncomfortable yet. It had been two weeks since she'd found the painting in the attic. Now she was standing on the front porch of Ryder's house watching Justin's white coupe drive off. Josh was in the car, along with his great-grandfather and Beatrice. The three were on their way to New Hampshire to visit Norman Gerard.

Justin traditionally went to see his brother once a year, after the crops were harvested. The choice of this time had become more a habit than a business necessity. He liked to oversee the planting, growing and harvesting of his crops, but he did very little of the actual work himself. At eighty, he was surprisingly spry. But a couple of years ago, he'd admitted that he wasn't as young as he used to be and he wanted more leisure time. So the majority of the physical labor of running his farm now rested in Hobart and Ryder's hands.

Thus, a few days ago when a letter from Norman had arrived expressing a desire to meet Josh, Justin had volunteered to reschedule his trip so that the boy could come along and not have to miss any of the following school year. As for Josh, he was anxious to meet all of the Gerards. When he'd been invited to accompany his great-grandfather, he pleaded with Emily to allow him. Knowing how much this meant to her son, she'd given her permission.

What hadn't occurred to her until afterward was that with Josh gone, she would be alone with Ryder. For a moment after this fact dawned on her, she experienced a rush of panic. Then it passed. Because both she and Ryder had been born and raised in Smytheshire, she'd known him all her life, although from a distance. He'd always unnerved her a little. To her he seemed larger and stronger than any other man. She'd also judged him to be decidedly stubborn and definitely authoritarian. But she'd also thought of him as being honest and hardworking. After living under his roof, she felt this assessment was pretty accurate. Even more, she was certain he would treat her fairly.

The realization that she actually trusted him had shaken her. *You shouldn't let your guard down so quickly,* her inner voice warned.

But standing on the porch with Ryder as they watched the white car making its way down the drive, she knew she had nothing to fear from the man beside her. *Mostly because he's barely aware of my existence,* she mused dryly, *and when he is he sees me as a necessary nuisance.*

"It's going to feel lonesome here without Josh." Ryder broke the silence between them as the car disappeared.

"Yes," Emily replied. "Really lonesome," she heard herself adding as a sense of isolation enveloped her. Realizing her tone and the emphasis she'd placed on her words had been less than flattering toward Ryder, she glanced at him. He was regarding her with an impatient scowl.

"I'd have moved into my grandfather's house for the time Josh will be gone, but that would've caused some unpleasant gossip. There might even have been speculations that would hinder the adoption proceedings," he said.

Emily had the feeling he would've preferred to be living in his grandfather's house than here with her. "We wouldn't want those proceedings to be delayed," she replied, promising herself she'd have her bags packed and be ready to leave the day they signed the papers.

"No, we wouldn't," Ryder confirmed. Then with a gesture at the barn, he said, "I've got chores to tend to."

Before she could utter a response, he was on his way down the steps. "Well, I've got chores, too," she muttered, going back into the house.

For the rest of the morning, she kept busy doing the laundry, vacuuming and ironing. When Ryder came in for lunch, she had soup and sandwiches ready.

It was a lunch just like any other lunch, she told herself as she sat down with him. But an uneasiness hung over the table. Until this moment she hadn't fully realized just how important Josh had been in keeping the tension at a minimum. Now it dawned on her that at mealtimes the conversation always involved him. She'd talk to him, or Ryder would talk to him, or they would both talk to him. But she and Ryder rarely conversed with each other. The thought of two weeks of this kind of silence was unbearable.

"How's the livestock?" she asked.

He looked at her, his expression one of indulgence. "Fine," he replied.

"Nothing interesting happening with them?" she persisted, determined to give this her best try. "None of them have learned any new tricks or done anything exciting?" Unable to believe she'd said that, she cringed inwardly. Well, she'd never been any good at small talk. She couldn't expect her first foray to be silver-tongued.

The hint of a smile curled one corner of his mouth. "Nope, not today."

She guessed he was silently laughing at her, and she couldn't blame him. "I feel like a fool," she admitted curtly. "But you make me nervous, and when I'm nervous I say dumb things." For a moment the realization she'd openly confessed his effect on her made her redden with embarrassment, then she scoffed at herself. She'd rather he knew she was nervous than think she was stupid.

The hint of the smile disappeared and he regarded her grimly. "You don't have to be afraid of me. I won't cause you any harm."

"I didn't say I was afraid of you," she replied impatiently. "I said you make me nervous." Suddenly worried that he might read more into her words than she wanted him to, she added, "I guess 'uncomfortable' would be a better description. I know you don't really want me here, and I don't like being where I'm not wanted."

Ryder drew a terse breath. "You're wrong. I do want you here," he said gruffly, then returned his attention to his food.

Emily studied him covertly as she forced herself to resume eating. She could have sworn there was honesty in his voice. The thought that he might actually like having her there crossed her mind and with it came a sudden rush of delight. *Idiot!* she chided herself. *It's not me he wants here, it's Josh and he has to put up with me to have my son.*

Admitting her attempt at conversation had led only to embarrassment, she made no further attempts during the remainder of the meal. A little later as she stood at the kitchen sink watching Ryder walk toward the barns, she frowned at herself. She was letting the man occupy too many of her thoughts.

"It's those ridiculous dreams," she hissed. "All right, all right, I'll admit it. He's attractive. But he's not attracted to me and I refuse to be attracted to him.'' Her jaw firmed with resolve, and she turned her full attention to cleaning the lunch dishes.

But halfway through the afternoon, she found herself pacing the living room. The house was clean and she had dinner planned. She considered running into town on the pretext of some errand or other, but that wouldn't help her relax. If she went into Smytheshire, she'd have to field not-so-subtle questions about how her marriage was working out.

She glanced around. There was no reason for her to feel the need to escape. Ryder wasn't even nearby. He was in the fields. Furthermore, she had the feeling he preferred to avoid her as much as possible. Because of that, she was sure he wouldn't come back to the house until dinnertime. "I could sit and read a book," she told herself. But sitting didn't appeal to her.

A sudden desire to bake an apple pie caused her to change direction and go into the kitchen. But as she pulled the cookbook out of its rack, she frowned at herself. Apple pie was the one dessert she'd made since she'd come here that Ryder had expressed a strong liking for. Pride refused to allow her to prepare something that might make him think she was cooking especially for him.

"I'll make oatmeal cookies. They're my favorite," she announced defiantly to the empty room.

And the smell of cookies baking did soothe her nerves. For a special touch, she added raisins to the second half of the batch. As she stood eating a warm cookie, she actually smiled. This was the first time in a long time she'd done something just for herself, and it felt good.

Then she heard the back door opening and abruptly the relaxed smile vanished and her tenseness returned.

"I thought I smelled oatmeal cookies," Ryder said, entering the kitchen and glancing at the table where the latest batch of cookies was cooling on a rack. "Mind if I have one?" he asked as he continued to the sink and began washing his hands.

"Help yourself," she replied, noting how the smell of sweat and dirt seemed to mingle enticingly with the sweet odors of her baking. *My mind must be really slipping,* she mocked herself.

Nodding, he dried his hands, then picked up four. "I've got to drive into town for a part for my tractor," he said, already heading for the door leading into the hall. "Be back in time for dinner."

She told herself he was merely busy, but she couldn't shake the feeling that he couldn't get way from her fast enough. She heard him go upstairs, then come back down. To her surprise, he came back through the kitchen and grabbed a few more cookies. She'd convinced herself that his show of delight in discovering she'd baked them had been merely a ruse to make her feel more welcome, but clearly he genuinely liked them.

She experienced a wave of pleasure at that, then scowled fiercely. She was only going to get hurt if she allowed herself to care even a small bit for him. The cookie she was eating suddenly lost its flavor....

Chapter Seven

Emily stood facing Ryder. It took all of her control to appear calm and indifferent. This was the third day of Josh's absence. As usual, Ryder had gone out before breakfast to do some chores. But after breakfast, instead of returning to the fields or the barns, he'd gone upstairs, bathed and changed into fresh clothes. When he'd come back downstairs, he'd been carrying an overnight bag.

"I'm going to be away for a couple of days," he was saying. "I've arranged for Les to come by and take care of the stock. He used to work for me before he married Vanessa and bought a farm of his own. He knows how I like things done."

Emily told herself she should feel relieved to be free of his company, but a nagging suspicion in the back of her mind had her stomach in knots. "Do you have a phone number you can leave in case I need to get in touch with you?'' she heard herself asking.

He shifted uncomfortably. "I'll give you a call later today and again tomorrow to make sure everything is all right."

The fact that he wouldn't leave a number increased her suspicions. "Have a good trip," she said stiffly.

"My father and Les will know how to take care of any emergencies," he assured her, then quickly left.

Watching through the living-room window as he drove away, Emily's jaw threatened to tremble. Her gut instinct told her that Hobart and Les had a number where Ryder could be reached. It also told her that Ryder was on his way to visit his mistress.

She drew a shaky breath. She shouldn't care. She knew he'd eventually go to the woman. She just hadn't expected it to upset her so much.

"I can't believe I'm letting this bother me," she chided herself turning away from the window and pacing across the room. "I was forewarned." Still, she felt a frustration so strong she had to fight back the urge to scream.

"Letting him affect me like this is definitely stupid!" she seethed. "We don't have a real marriage. I knew he had a mistress. I shouldn't care if he goes to see her!"

She paced back across the room. "I find the man attractive, that's all. But I'm the last woman in the world he wants to be with. He's made it perfectly clear during these past weeks that he prefers to keep a distance between us. And that would be for the best. A physical relationship between me and Ryder would only complicate the situation. This marriage isn't going to last. It's strictly a short-term deal.''

Her jaw hardened. "He's welcome to go visit his mistress whenever he pleases."

The sensation of something wet trailing down her cheek caught her attention. To her chagrin, she realized her eyes were brimming with tears. She was crying over Ryder Gerard! Angrily she brushed them away. The urge to scream grew stronger. Instead, her body stiffened, she squeezed her hands into tight fists and clenched her teeth. "I will *not* behave like a fool over a man, especially not over Ryder Gerard!"

The scowl on Ryder's face deepened as he pulled out onto the main road. "Going to Plainfield isn't going to solve the problem," he muttered.

It was, however, a safer solution than the one that had been tormenting him for the past few days, he argued back.

"Damn!" he growled in frustration.

At the sound of a vehicle approaching, Emily glanced out the window. If it was Les, she was going to go upstairs and hide out in her room. She knew it was cowardly, but she had no desire to face her brother-in-law, especially since she was sure he knew where Ryder had gone. But it wasn't Les's Jeep she saw coming. It was Ryder's blue Chevy.

As he parked beside his pickup, she started toward the back of the house. She refused to face him a second time this morning. She'd hide out in the kitchen until he left again.

But as she stood at the counter staring out the back window, trying to concentrate on the scene beyond and ignore Ryder's presence in the house, she heard his booted footsteps coming down the hall. *I should have gone up to my room,* she berated herself. He never would have gone there. He avoided that room like the plague.

As the door opened, she turned to face him. She'd meant to simply issue an indifferent, mildly surprised hello as if she hadn't been aware of his return, then head for her room. Instead, she heard herself say dryly, "Forget to take a snack to keep your energy up on the drive to Plainfield?"

Ryder had stopped a couple of feet into the room. Now he stood watching her, his expression shuttered.

It occurred to Emily she might have been wrong about his destination. But she was pretty sure she wasn't. Besides, even if she was wrong this time, he was bound to take off to see his mistress sooner or later. Deciding she'd rather have this part of their relationship out in the open than eating away inside of her, she said, "My brother came by to see me before the wedding. He thought I should know about your mistress."

Ryder scowled. "I thought I'd been more discreet."

Realizing she'd hoped he'd tell her her brother had lied, Emily's stomach knotted more tightly. "It's hard to keep anything in this town a secret."

"That's true," Ryder agreed grudgingly.

He was studying her with a scrutiny that was causing her nerves to come close to breaking. "Why did you come back?" she asked, hoping he would take care of whatever errand he had returned to do and leave before she said something that might really embarrass her.

"Probably to get my face slapped," he replied. "But I didn't think it was fair to be with one woman when I wanted to be with another."

Before Emily could move, he'd crossed the room. His hands closed around her upper arms, and in the next instant she felt his lips on hers. Her body stiffened, prepared for battle. Granted, she was attracted to him, but she would not allow herself to be misused again.

To her surprise, his kiss wasn't brutal or demanding. Although it was firm, it was also gently coaxing as if tempting her to participate. He also loosened his hold on her arms.

As she felt his grip slacken, she told herself that the smart thing to do would be to move away from him. But before she could make her body respond, his strong callused hands began to travel caressingly upward over her shoulders.

Shaken by the searing trail left by his touch, she stood immobile as his hands ended their travels by cupping her face. She felt the kiss lighten and thought he was ending it. Regret washed over her. But instead of abruptly breaking the contact, he paused and nibbled her lip. Then, like putting a period at the end of a sentence, he kissed her firmly one more time and released her, taking two steps back.

The feel of his hands and lips lingered on Emily's skin as she stood watching him. She tried to think of something to say, but was afraid if she did attempt to speak, the words would come out in a jumble.

"It's your move, Emily," Ryder said. "You're an appetizing woman. Living under the same roof with you has been a strain. And there have been moments when I could swear I've seen you looking at me with, shall we say, interest in your eyes. I've been telling myself it would be best if we kept our relationship uninvolved. But the truth is I can't go running off to Plainfield every time the mood strikes me, and it's been striking me a heck of a lot lately. But I won't force myself on you. I'm leaving it up to you. I can stay here or I can go to Plainfield."

At least he was blunt about what he wanted, she thought. "I've always known you were nothing but trouble, Ryder Gerard," she said. Her rational side was ordering her to send him on his way. But she wasn't feeling rational. Her gaze was riveted on him. She wanted to run her hands over his shoulders to feel their solid strength. "And you're right. I thought I was immune to lusty cravings but I was wrong. I guess I'm only human."

One corner of his mouth quirked into a smile. "We are married. We might as well give in to our human side and get some enjoyment out of this arrangement."

He was making it clear that what happened between them would be nothing more than physical, Emily noted. But then that was all it would be to her as well, she assured herself. Even more importantly, being with him might put an end to her erotic fantasies and ease the strain she'd been feeling. In fact, just being with him once would probably cure her of wanting him anywhere near her, she reasoned. Then she could send him to Plainfield with her best wishes.

She gave what she hoped was an indifferent shrug. "Might as well see if we're compatible."

The brown of his eyes darkened with purpose. "And now is as good a time as any," he said, moving toward her.

Show a little hesitation, Emily ordered herself. Don't behave totally wantonly. But instead, she heard herself saying, "Yes, as good a time as any."

The heat in his eyes increased. Reaching her, he cupped her face. His fingers raked into her hair and each sent its own trail of fire weaving through her. Then his mouth found hers.

This time there was a hunger in his kiss. She expected to feel a certain amount of trepidation, but instead, she felt a hunger that matched his. Her hands came up to move exploringly over his chest; she wanted to see if he was as sturdy as she'd imagined. He was, and a thrill of excitement raced through her.

His kiss lightened. He nibbled teasingly at her lips, then lifted his head away. She opened her eyes to find him looking down at her, an expression of satisfaction on his face.

I'm being too easy, she scolded herself. But even as her mind ordered her to show a little resistance, his hands left her face to travel caressingly down her back, and her body melted against his. As he reached her hips and drew her hard against him, she felt the power of his need, and an answering passion burned within her.

"You're a strain on a man's control," he said raggedly. "I want you here and now."

The intensity of her willingness to allow him that wish shocked her. She'd never felt such a craving for anything before. "I've spent a lot of years wondering what having a willing relationship with a man would be like," she heard herself saying huskily. "And right now my curiosity is at its peak."

He grinned. "I'll be happy to satisfy it."

Her body suddenly stiffened, fear mingling with anticipation as he released her and stepped back. Then she reached out and began to unbutton his shirt. But as she finished with the first button and moved to the second, he caught her by the wrists.

"As much as I'd like to continue this without interruption, we're going to do this where we'll be comfortable," he said, and in the next instant Emily found herself being hoisted over his shoulder.

As he carried her up the stairs, he ran one hand along her leg. "You're making me crazy," she warned as the fires he'd already started burned even hotter.

"Good," he replied, giving her butt a playful slap. Then he applied himself to pulling off her shoes and socks and dropping them along the hallway as he continued to his room.

By the time he stood her on the floor beside his bed, she was ready to rip his clothes off him. "I've obviously delayed having a physical relationship much too long," she said, surprised she could put a coherent sentence together.

"I'll try not to disappoint you," he promised as he began to unbutton her blouse.

Too impatient to wait, Emily worked at getting his clothes off him while he stripped her of hers. But her fingers moved clumsily and he was already stripping her of her jeans when she had gotten only as far as pulling at the snap of his. "Unfair," she teased with a nervous laugh. "You had a belt I had to get rid of."

He grinned down at her. "Time for you to get off your feet." Lifting her, he tossed her playfully onto the bed. A rush of shyness suddenly washed over her. It's a little late for that, she thought. Still, aloud, she said, "Meet you under the covers."

"Just one more thing first," he replied, and before she could move, he'd caught the waistband of her panties and they came sliding off.

For a moment she lay frozen, looking up at him. A tint of embarrassment spread over her. This was the first time she'd ever been totally naked in front of a man, and the sudden fear of rejection washed over her. But the heat of his gaze left no doubt that he liked what he saw, and delight washed away her embarrassment.

As he turned to finish taking off his clothes, she quickly tossed back the bedspread and slipped under the sheet. When she glanced back toward him, she saw he'd moved to his dresser and realized he was taking precautions. She wasn't surprised. Ryder Gerard was one of the most thorough men she'd ever met. And he always seemed to remain in control.

On the other hand, I am totally out of control, she thought frantically. She was crazy to be doing this, her inner voice screamed at her. But before she could heed the warning, he joined her, and his touch reignited a fire that threatened to consume her unless she allowed him to save her.

"Ryder, please," she gasped pleadingly.

"Gladly," he growled.

Emily was startled at the newness as he claimed her. Then a sense of being complete washed over her and she became lost in a world of ecstasy.

Emily lay watching Ryder. He had held her until her breathing had returned to normal, then he'd said, "Be back in a minute."

As he'd left the bed she'd wondered if she should get up and leave the room. She had no idea what the protocol for an affair was. Of course this wasn't exactly an affair. They were married. The way he'd said he'd be right back indicated he expected her to still be there when he returned, she reasoned. She shifted her gaze to the ceiling. She wasn't used to being so indecisive, but then, she'd never expected to find herself in Ryder Gerard's bed. The bed shifted and she knew he was back.

"I enjoyed your company," he said, levering himself up on an elbow and looking down at her, his expression guarded.

"I enjoyed your company, too," she replied honestly.

His gaze narrowed. "No regrets?"

I've probably just done a very foolish thing, she thought, even as she wished for a repeat performance. But she refused to regret her behavior. "No," she answered. Suddenly it occurred to her that he might be wishing he'd gone on to Plainfield. "What about you?" she forced herself to ask. "Are you sorry you stayed here?"

He grinned crookedly. "No." Leaning down, he kissed her lightly.

Emily felt the flames of desire begin to ignite once again, but then Ryder pulled away from her.

"I'm exhausted," he said gruffly. "Been spending too many restless nights. Now I'm relaxed. I hope you don't mind if I go to sleep." Yawning, he eased himself back onto his pillow.

When he'd returned to the bed, he'd lain down so that his body was not touching hers. Now as he lay back, there was more than a foot of space separating them.

A rush of disappointment swept through her. Obviously she didn't spark a fire in him the way he did in her. *Oh well, what I feel is just physical, anyway,* she told herself. *After a couple of more times, I'll probably be bored by the whole business.*

She turned to look at him. He was breathing evenly and quietly. He was already asleep! Irritated with herself for feeling piqued, she eased out of bed. Deciding she didn't want to disturb him, she began gathering up her clothes to take them into her room to dress.

But as she started to leave, the bedroom door swung shut. She glanced toward the open windows. The curtains were hanging quietly. Whatever breeze had caught the door had quickly died down. Turning to see if the noise had disturbed Ryder, she saw him watching her.

"Guess I wasn't as sleepy as I thought," he said, leaving the bed and moving toward her.

The sight of him immediately stirred the embers of desire within her. She'd never thought of herself as being so wanton, but he certainly had a way of bringing out that side of her.

"Stay a while longer," he coaxed, reaching her and running his hands caressingly along the curve of her hip.

His rough palms sent currents of heated excitement racing through her. *Show a little resistance,* her inner voice ordered, but again her body refused to obey. The clothes fell from her hands. "If you're sure you're not too tired," she said, letting her body lightly press against his.

"I'm definitely not too tired," he assured her, impatience flickering in his eyes as his hold on her tightened.

"In that case, I suppose I could stay a while longer," she replied, her lips gently brushing his as she spoke. She'd never believed she could banter with a man like this, but at the moment the words seemed to come naturally.

Ryder lifted her into his arms. He kissed her on the shoulder, then moved lower as he carried her back to the bed.

Emily lay watching Ryder sleep. The second time he'd made love to her had been as exciting as the first. She'd hoped it would be a little less. Her gaze shifted to the door. She didn't know whether to feel grateful to it for slamming shut and waking him, or to curse it. *My mind's a muddle,* she wailed silently. Deciding she needed to put some distance between her and Ryder, she eased out of bed, regathered her clothes and quietly left the room.

Ryder opened his eyes as the door closed behind Emily. Taking her to his bed was probably the stupidest thing he'd ever done, he told himself. He'd promised himself he'd stay as far away from her as possible. "Well, I sure broke that promise," he growled under his breath.

Shifting onto his side, he reached for the phone. He had to call Plainfield and let Loretta know he wouldn't be coming. He knew she wouldn't mind. She'd always been adamant about neither of them feeling bound to the other. She'd been a good friend and a comfortable companion, and he'd miss their conversations. But there'd never been any real passion between them.

Emily, on the other hand, ignited his passion but he'd never describe her as a comfortable companion. *She's dangerous*, he warned himself for the umpteenth time. *But what was done was done.*

Chapter Eight

As Emily set the sandwich she'd made for Ryder's lunch on the kitchen table, she glanced indecisively toward the door leading to the hall. For the past hour she'd been debating whether or not to wake him. Uncertainty about facing him now that they'd been intimate pervaded her. They hadn't been on what she could call friendly terms before she'd accepted his invitation to join him in his bed. There'd been merely an air of social politeness between them. *I should act casual and let him set the tone,* she decided finally.

Her body wasn't making this decision easy. She wanted to return to his bedroom all right, but getting him out of bed wasn't what she had in mind. "If I give in to this craving, he'll think I'm utterly wanton," she admonished herself.

A sudden wave of anxiety shook her. He might even begin to wonder if Hallam's version of the night Josh was conceived was true. She'd spent a lot of years telling herself she didn't care what anyone thought of her. Now she was forced to admit she cared very much.

"Afternoon."

Emily stiffened as Ryder strode into the kitchen. *Act naturally,* she ordered herself. "Your timing is perfect," she said with forced nonchalance.

"I thought we both had very good timing," he replied.

She saw the heat in his eyes and an answering heat curled through her. Abruptly Hallam's image entered her mind and a chill vanquished the warmth. "I wasn't like that with your brother," she blurted. "I didn't participate willingly. I told you the truth about what happened that night."

He regarded her levelly. "I believe you."

Emily's entire body had tensed. She'd already admitted that other people's opinions of her mattered. But until this moment, she'd never realized just how much she cared about Ryder's opinion. The honesty in his voice brought a rush of relief. Forcing Hallam out of her mind, she motioned toward the table. "Your lunch is ready."

He smiled lazily. "Thanks, I'm starved."

Emily knew that if they were truly lovers, she would have returned his smile and said something about an exerting morning. But the words stuck in her throat. All she could manage was a stilted, "Me, too."

Ryder's easy smile faded and a silence descended over the table as they seated themselves and began to eat. *Say something,* she ordered herself as she forced a bite of sandwich down, but nothing came. Glancing at Ryder, she caught him studying her guardedly. *He's probably wishing he'd gone to Plainfield,* she thought.

"I'm not very good at banter," she said abruptly.

"I noticed," he replied, an edge of impatience in his voice. Downing his glass of iced tea, he rose. "I've got work to do."

As he left she was sure he was regretting having stayed. Again she found herself wanting to scream in frustration. Instead, she cleaned up the dishes and went out and hoed the vegetable garden she'd planted behind the house.

During dinner, she and Ryder both made attempts at small talk. She asked him about his crops. He asked her about her garden. They speculated about how the visit with Norman was going. But Emily was sure she saw flashes of discomfort escape from behind his polite facade.

With each passing moment, she grew more certain he was wishing the morning had never happened. By the time the meal ended, her nerves were close to snapping. "Why don't you go read the newspaper and relax? I can clean up the dishes on my own," she said with dismissal when he began helping her clear the table.

For a second, he looked as if he was going to argue, then he said, "I have some paperwork I need to do."

She heard him go into his study and close the door. She groaned as the tension within the walls of the house seemed to multiply a hundredfold. *We've managed to make a difficult situation even worse,* she admonished herself as she washed the plates. *The best thing would be to forget what happened.*

But forgetting wasn't easy, she lamented later that night. Pleading exhaustion, she'd gone up to her room early. For an hour she'd tried reading, but the words kept blurring in front of her eyes as memories of Ryder's lovemaking taunted her.

Giving up, she turned off her light and tried to sleep. But lying there in the dark, she could almost feel his hands moving caressingly over her and frustration filled her. *I've led too sheltered a life,* she decided. If she'd had more experience with men, she'd have been able to put Ryder out of her mind. But then, she'd never been attracted to any man before him. *Obviously, I'm one of those women for whom men are nothing but trouble,* she concluded haplessly.

Glancing at the clock, she noticed it was nearly eleven-thirty. She'd been tossing and turning for more than an hour. Feeling as if the walls of the room were closing in on her, she rose and pulled on her robe.

She'd heard Ryder go to bed an hour ago. She could roam freely around the house now. Still, as she went downstairs, the feeling of being stifled prevailed. Stepping out onto the front porch, she drew in a deep breath of the warm summer air. The scent of hay reminded her of Ryder as he looked when he came in from the fields. She'd told herself she didn't care if he'd already grown bored with her. Now she was forced to admit that was a lie. The sting of rejection was sharp and strong. She'd made a terrible mistake giving in to her emotions this morning.

"Having trouble sleeping?"

Emily jerked around to discover Ryder coming out onto the porch. He was dressed only in a pair of jeans, and the sight of his bare chest caused the embers of desire to again burn. *Fool!* she chided herself, taking a step back to keep several feet between them.

Ryder scowled. "I'm not my brother. You don't have to worry about me forcing myself on you."

The impatience in his voice caused her already taut nerves to snap. "I'm not afraid of that. You've made it clear you're not interested in me any longer."

"I thought maybe *you* were regretting this morning," he replied. "You've been even more tense than usual." The scowl on his face deepened. "And maybe I have been a little worried that we made a mistake." His gaze narrowed on her. "But I'm still interested."

The admission that he was still interested brought a rush of pleasure. As a reason for his concern that they might have made a mistake dawned on her, she faced him levelly. "If you're thinking that just because we've been intimate I'm going to start getting romantic notions and think this marriage might be a forever one, don't. What happened between us was nothing more than two adults giving in to physical needs."

"It would be best to keep romantic notions out of our relationship," Ryder said. Continuing to allow the distance between them, he added, "My bed feels real lonely."

Clearly he was leaving the decision about continuing their intimacy up to her. Again, she told herself to show some restraint. Instead, she heard herself admitting, "Mine, too."

He extended his hand toward her. "I have a solution."

"I guessed you might," she replied. Even as her inner voice warned her she could be asking for real trouble, she moved toward him. What harm could indulging in a little physical pleasure cause? she reasoned as his hand encased hers and the warmth of the contact spread up her arm and through her body.

The next morning, as she lay beside a still-sleeping Ryder, Emily thought about his lovemaking. He'd proved to be a very thorough, very accommodating lover. It occurred to her that his mistress must be missing his company. A sudden sharp jab of what felt like jealousy pierced her. *I don't really care for him,* she assured herself. *All I feel is physical attraction.* Still, she abruptly pushed the thoughts of the other woman from her mind.

"Morning," Ryder said, lazily shifting onto his side as he opened his eyes.

Even the dark stubble of beard on his face was inviting to the touch, she thought. It wasn't fair that he looked so appealing! *I'm just feeling this way because this is all so new to me,* she reasoned. *A couple of more mornings like this and I'll probably just think he needs a shave.* Right now, though, she was wondering how that stubble would feel against the palm of her hand and how his lips would taste. . . .

"If you keep looking at me like that, we're never going to get out of this bed," he warned huskily.

Emily blushed. She hadn't meant for her thoughts to show so openly. "I'll go start the coffee," she said, and moved to throw off the covers.

Ryder's hand closed around her arm. "There's no need to rush."

"I do hate to rush," she replied, allowing him to pull her toward him.

He grinned and her blush deepened as she realized the double entendre of her words. "Then I promise to move slowly," he said.

His hand was caressing her body. She wanted to say something clever, but his touch made thinking nearly impossible. Then his actions became more possessive and her breath locked in her lungs. Forgetting about making conversation, she brushed her cheek against his to test the feel of his morning stubble. The effect was enticing, and all thoughts but those of enjoying this moment vanished.

"I want you to move into my room," Ryder said as they sat in the kitchen eating breakfast a little later. "I'm not interested in making appointments when I want to see you or padding across the hall in the middle of the night playing musical beds."

Emily admitted to herself that she wanted to continue their physical relationship, but she had one serious reservation. "What will we tell Josh?"

"My guess is he won't ask," Ryder replied. "He wants this marriage to work. He'll be glad we're behaving like husband and wife."

"My son doesn't simply make assumptions," Emily pointed out. "His questions might be subtle, but he'll ask." Self-consciousness crept into her voice. "I'd rather not tell him we're simply having a short-term affair, but I don't want to lie to him, either."

"We'll tell him we're trying to make the best of our marriage," Ryder said. "That won't be lying or making any promises we don't intend to keep."

"Agreed," Emily replied with relief. But the relief was short-lived. There was one other matter her pride insisted be faced. "I have one restriction about our new arrangement."

Ryder raised a quizzical eyebrow.

"As long as we're sharing the same bed, I expect fidelity." As the words came out her body tensed as if preparing for a physical blow.

Ryder shrugged. "That seems fair."

Surprised he'd so easily agreed, Emily had to fight to keep from staring at him. She'd thought her demand might cause him to think twice about continuing their new relationship. "What about your friend in Plainfield?" she asked bluntly, too nervous to be subtle.

"She'd agree with you," he said. "When I called her yesterday to tell her I wasn't coming, she admitted that my being a married man made her uncomfortable. She has a moral code she lives by. She said that after I called the first time to say I was coming, she got to thinking about how she'd have felt if her husband had ever cheated on her. She concluded she wouldn't have liked it. And she didn't like thinking of herself as the other woman. She said she was planning to send me on my way when I showed up."

"I'm sorry," she said. To herself, Emily confessed that she wasn't really sorry, but she felt she should say something.

"No reason to be," he replied. "She also told me she was beginning to be a bit bored with her life. She said I'd been neglecting her too much and she's been thinking about finding someone who would spend more time with her. I got the impression she was considering looking for a man who was interested in marriage." He grinned thoughtfully. "In fact, I'm sure she already has someone picked out. Her old high-school sweetheart was recently widowed. I've always had the feeling that flame never quite died."

Emily noticed there was not even the slightest hint of regret in his voice. "You don't sound as if you mind losing her," she observed.

"We're still friends," he replied, as if that was all that was important to him.

Emily studied him narrowly. "A person could get the impression you only enter into relationships where there's no romantic involvement. Or has the right woman just never come along?" Mentally she gasped as she realized what she'd said. But now that she had, she found herself very interested in his answer.

His expression became shuttered. "Romantic involvements can lead to complications that cause trouble for both parties. I prefer not to invite trouble when possible."

"Trouble is something I prefer to live without myself," she replied.

But a little later, as she watched Ryder walking toward the barn, it occurred to her that he was trouble personified. *However, as long as I don't go getting any foolish romantic notions, everything will work out just fine,* she assured herself.

Even though she and Ryder had agreed on what to tell Josh, Emily was nervous the day her son returned. She'd insisted that Justin and Beatrice stay for lunch. During the meal, the conversation revolved around their visit to Norman Gerard. Almost immediately after they'd eaten, Justin and Beatrice had pleaded exhaustion from their long drive and gone home. Josh had wanted to go see his horse, and he and Ryder had gone out to the barn, leaving Emily alone in the house.

As she cleaned up the lunch dishes, she wondered how she should broach the subject of her new sleeping arrangements. Josh had to be told. She didn't want him to simply notice the change without any warning.

"Ryder tells me that the two of you are working at this marriage," Josh's voice sounded unexpectedly from behind her.

She turned to find her son grinning at her. Clearly, Ryder had already explained the new arrangements to the boy. "We're making the best of it," she replied.

His grin broadened. "I'm glad. He can be a little rough around the edges sometimes, but I knew you'd learn to like him if you gave him half a chance."

Deceiving her son caused Emily some guilt. But if she told him the truth, he might think she was behaving wantonly and she didn't want that. Instead, she said, "Ryder does have his good qualities."

A prickling on the side of her neck caused her to look toward the door. Ryder was standing there.

"I think you have some unpacking to do," he said to Josh.

The boy nodded and, giving his mother a final grin, he headed for his room.

"Never thought I'd hear you admitting I might have a few good qualities," Ryder said, continuing to study Emily. "Did you mean it, or was that just for Josh's sake?"

His manner was noncommittal, but she had the feeling her answer mattered. "I meant it," she replied honestly.

His jaw tensed. "I know I can't make up for the damage my brother did to your life. But I am trying."

Emily berated herself. For one brief moment, she'd thought he really cared how she felt about him. But what he cared about was righting a wrong. *Someday I'll find a man who cares about me,* she told herself, *but it wasn't going to be Ryder Gerard.*

In spite of Josh's easy acceptance of her intimacy with Ryder, Emily couldn't relax. That night, when she went up to bed, she was decidedly on edge. Hoping to relax, she took a hot shower. But as she dried herself, the thought of her son down the hall caused her muscles to tense again. In spite of the fact that this bathroom was part of the master bedroom suite thus ensuring her privacy, she wrapped a towel around herself before entering the adjoining bedroom.

"I think we need to talk."

Her body stiffened at the sound of Ryder's voice. Looking in the direction from which it had come, she saw him seated in the upholstered chair by the window. Her hand went up to make certain the towel was securely fastened.

A flicker of anger flashed across his face. "It's a little late to worry about modesty," he said curtly.

She wanted to say something, but no words came. He had every right to feel impatient with her. Still she continued to hold the towel firmly in place.

He regarded her coolly. "Do you want to move out?"

The word *yes* formed in her mind. But even as it was taking shape, the desire to be in his arms, to feel the warmth of his body, threatened to overwhelm her. "No," she confessed tightly.

The brown of his eyes darkened and he smiled. "I'm glad to hear that."

Normally when he looked at her that way, her body flamed. She knew he was planning to make love to her, and this should have caused a wave of excited expectation. Instead, she felt cold and rigid. As he rose and approached her, her muscles tightened even more.

Reaching her, he cupped her face in his hands and kissed her. She willed herself to relax, but couldn't. Even the heat of his touch had no soothing effect.

Taking a step back, he frowned down at her. "You feel as stiff as a board." His frown deepened. "I prefer my women soft and willing."

Emily's nerves broke. "I realize that for you this—" she waved her hand around the room "—is just a natural part of life. That's all right for a man. But no matter how much people keep saying it isn't so, there's still a double standard. Men are supposed to be lusty. Women are supposed to show some restraint, some control."

Frustration etched itself into her features. "I can't stop thinking about how Josh will feel about me if he should ever discover that all you and I are doing is satisfying physical cravings—that we're just having an affair we have no intention of continuing."

"You're not giving your son enough credit. I'm sure Josh understands human needs," he replied.

She scowled at him. "*You* don't understand. Sons view their mothers differently from other women. Mothers aren't supposed to have the same weaknesses. We're supposed to be pure."

He shook his head at her logic. "I think you're being a bit too hard on yourself."

"Maybe," she conceded with a shaky breath. The fear in her eyes increased. "But if Josh ever turned against me, I couldn't handle that. He's all I have."

"Josh loves you," Ryder said. "When a person loves someone, they'll overlook and forgive a great deal. Besides, you're doing nothing wrong or even immoral. We're married and we're behaving like two adults."

"I know," she conceded. Bitterness entered her voice. "But I'm a little insecure when it comes to being loved. In my case, I never expect it to last." She colored at the admission. She never talked openly to people about her innermost fears, and here she was telling Ryder Gerard things she didn't like admitting even to herself.

Ryder's jaw hardened. "Real love isn't something that comes and goes with the breeze. It's more like an oak that survives every storm and continues to grow and strengthen."

It occurred to Emily that if Ryder ever loved a woman, he would stand beside her through the fires of hell. The sudden powerful wish that she could be that woman shook her. *I'm not and never will be,* she reminded herself. *And,* she added curtly, *I don't need or want him or any man to lean on.*

Aloud she said cynically, "That's very poetic for a man who doesn't believe in romantic attachments."

He shrugged. "It's not that I don't believe in them. My mother and father and my grandparents had marriages based on strong bonds of love. I'm just not so sure how to tell when the feelings are real or when they're so weak they'll break with the slightest gust of wind."

The thought flashed through her mind that perhaps there *was* a possibility he could learn to care for her. "I suppose sometimes a person just has to take a chance," she heard herself saying.

A coolness descended over his features. "There are times when the risk can be too great."

The determination in his eyes made it clear he never intended to take that risk. And even if he did, she wasn't the woman who would inspire him to. "You could be right about that," she admitted. She'd vowed a dozen times never to allow herself to develop an emotional attachment to him. Now she reaffirmed that vow.

"If I promise not to touch you until you have time to adjust to having Josh in the house again, will you relax?" he asked, returning their conversation to its original topic.

"I'll try," she replied, silently laughing at herself. The reason she was still in this room was that, in spite of her fears, their intimacy had such a strong hold on her. It was like a hunger that had to be fed. He, however, obviously didn't feel the same, she thought, noting the casual way he'd offered to keep his hands off of her. *That's because he's used to intimate relationships, and I'm not,* she told herself. *When the newness wears off, I'll be just as blasé.*

He nodded his acceptance of her decision, then went into the bathroom.

Emily heard him turning on the shower as she pulled on a nightgown and climbed into the king-size bed. Shifting onto her side, she lay staring at his pillow. He didn't really care if she was there or not. He'd offered her the option of moving back into her own room. Now he'd promised to stay away from her until she wanted him back. A hurtful thought suddenly crossed her mind. Maybe he was already tired of her. Maybe he'd prefer her to move back into her room. Her body stiffened with pride, and she tossed off the sheet and rose.

When Ryder came out of the bathroom a few minutes later, she was sitting in the chair he'd occupied, waiting for him. She'd assured herself she was steeled against him, but the sight of his naked body caused the fires of passion to blaze. *He makes me feel absolutely lecherous,* she wailed silently. She tried telling herself that he'd simply awakened the woman in her, but when she tried thinking of other men she knew they left her cold. *And you leave him cold,* she reminded herself. To her relief, this thought caused her ardor to dampen.

"I thought you promised you'd try to relax," he said, a note of impatience in his voice.

"It occurred to me you might have offered to allow me to move back to my own room because that's what you *want* me to do." She faced him defiantly. "If you're tired of me, just say so."

The impatience in his face intensified. Crossing the room in long strides, he grasped her by the upper arms and pulled her to her feet. "I am not tired of you," he growled. "I wish I was. It would've saved me from having to take that damn cold shower. I'm merely trying to live up to my part of our bargain by not putting any demands on you."

She couldn't blame him for being exasperated with her. She was exasperated with herself. "I'm sorry," she said.

His hold on her arms loosened and, in a gentle massaging motion, he worked his hands upward to her shoulders. "You could make amends," he said gruffly.

His touch was warm and enticing. Looking up into his face, she read the desire in the dark depths of his eyes. As an answering fire flamed within her, she replied, "I suppose I should."

I deserve to have some pleasure in life, she reasoned as he bent to kiss her. When their lips met, she shut out thoughts of the world beyond their bedroom door.

Chapter Nine

Emily reined in her horse as Ryder brought his to a stop. It was late October, and the day had the crisp feel of winter in the air.

"Been thinking I'd clear a few acres here," Ryder said, looking out over the wooded landscape. "Josh shows a real ability with horses. We'll build a row of stables over there." He pointed to his left. "I'm planning on enough to house the three horses we already have and a few more. Then I'll buy a couple of high-quality mares and a stallion. There's always a market for good horses." He turned toward her. "What do you think? Will Josh like the idea of being a horse breeder?"

"I know he'll like it," she replied, forcing a smile. Inwardly she felt like an idiot. When Ryder had waited until Josh had gone off to school and then asked her to go riding, she felt like a teenager on her first date.

Until today, she and Ryder had never gone riding alone. Josh had always been with them. And he still was, she thought dryly.

Ryder smiled at her words of approval. "Sam Marley said he'd buy the timber. He can have his crew here tomorrow."

Nudging his horse into a walk, he began a final inspection of the land he planned to have cleared. As they rode, he pointed out where he thought he'd build the corrals and talked about how much land they should clear and fence for grazing, giving the horses room to run and roam.

Emily rode beside him, only half listening. She was pleased Ryder took such a strong interest in Josh. He was generous, too. When Josh wanted to borrow Ryder's car, Ryder nearly always let him have it. He also paid Josh a salary for work done on the farm.

"The boy should have his own money," he'd told Emily.

But to her relief, Ryder didn't spoil Josh, either. He disciplined him when the boy behaved irresponsibly. Emily vividly remembered the first time Josh and Ryder had quarreled. It had been a hot August day. Josh had come stomping into the house and gone up to his room without a word. She'd known from the hurt angry look on his face that something was terribly wrong.

She'd gone up to his room to find him glowering out the window. "You want to tell me what's going on?" she asked worriedly.

"Ryder says I have to stick around after lunch and fix the corral gate all by myself. I told him I'd do it tomorrow. I explained I'd made plans to meet a bunch of friends down by the river to go swimming this afternoon. But he says I have to fix the gate today," he replied curtly, continuing to glare out the window.

Emily's shoulders straightened. Ryder had no right to order Josh around like that. Josh wasn't his slave. "You keep your plans. I'll have a talk with Ryder." Furious that Ryder would treat Josh so harshly, she started to leave Josh's room to go in search of the man and give him a piece of her mind. In a way, she admitted, this was almost a relief. She'd been trying to find some fault with him that would make keeping an emotional distance easier.

"Wait!" Josh called before she reached the door. When she turned back toward him, she saw a contrite expression on his face. "I guess I left a little out," he said stiffly. "Fixing the corral is sort of a punishment. I left some equipment out last night. We worked late and I was in a hurry to meet the guys. I forgot about it." A defensiveness entered his voice. "People do forget once in a while. I'm not perfect."

Emily stood watching her son indecisively. She had to admit that Ryder's punishing Josh bothered her. Until now she'd been both mother and father to her son. Disciplining him had been her domain. But to be fair, the man was in the right. "Sort of like when I used to make you clean up your room when you misbehaved," she said.

"Yeah," Josh conceded. Grudgingly he added, "And he's right. Equipment is expensive and it could have been damaged." His jaw formed a firm line. "I'll stick around and fix the corral." Stalking past her, he left the house.

She was in the kitchen when Ryder had come looking for her a few minutes later. "Thought I should let you vent your anger," he said. "I figured you'd resent my disciplining Josh. But you might as well know, since I'm taking on the role of the boy's father, I'm going to do what I think is right."

"I was upset at first," Emily admitted. "But I've been thinking about it, and as long as you're fair, then I think you should have some say in his upbringing."

He looked surprised. "You've proven to be a much more reasonable woman than I ever thought you would be."

"I guess we both have a lot to learn about each other," she replied, finding herself wanting to know all there was to know about him.

"Guess so," he returned.

Emily noticed his guard suddenly come up, and without any further conversation, he headed for the door. Obviously he wasn't interested in either of them learning too much about each other, she mused dryly as she watched him leave. But then, he'd made it clear from the start he planned to keep their relationship on a superficial level.

Lunch has been a solemn meal, with little said among the three. Josh was contrite, but Ryder's face was set. Once, she caught him glancing surreptitiously toward Josh, a shadow of uneasiness in his eyes.

Emily was well acquainted with the uneasiness Ryder was feeling. He was standing his ground because it was the right thing to do, yet he was worried about Josh's holding a grudge. Ryder, Emily was forced to admit, was good father material. Realizing that this was no time for small talk, she remained calm but silent during the meal.

While she'd washed the dishes, though, she couldn't help feeling sorry for Josh. He'd had a rough time this past year and she wanted him to have some fun. She quickly finished the dishes, then headed out to the corral to offer her help. If they fixed the gate soon enough, he could still spend the major portion of the afternoon with his friends.

But as she neared the corral, she saw Ryder coming out of the barn and heading toward Josh. "Got to thinking this gate was more of a two-man job," he said as he reached the teenager.

"Thanks," she heard Josh reply. His voice sounded repentant as he added, "I'm sorry about leaving the equipment out."

Emily saw Ryder nod and give the boy a pat on the shoulder. Josh's expression relaxed and she knew the two had made their peace.

Fairly certain that neither had noticed her, Emily had turned and gone back to the house. Working together, Ryder and Josh finished the gate quickly and Josh had been able to spend the majority of the afternoon with his friends.

"I hope my making long-term plans for Josh doesn't bother you," Ryder said, jerking Emily's mind back to the present. "But I'm taking my responsibilities as his father seriously."

Emily's gaze swung to him. "I know you care about Josh. I can't find any fault with your plans."

Ryder's gaze narrowed on her. "I do care about the boy." For a moment a look of indecision shadowed his features, then it was replaced with resolve. "I've grown used to having both of you around," he said. "I was wondering if you'd consider staying after the adoption is complete. We make a pretty good three-some."

Emily wanted to believe he really wanted her to re-main. But she'd seen his hesitation before making this offer. Her shoulders squared. "You don't have invite me to stay simply to assure yourself access to Josh. I won't keep him away."

"I'm not just thinking about Josh," he said, a gruffness entering his voice. "I enjoy your com-pany."

Delight flowed through Emily. *Don't start thinking he means anything deeper than the physical pleasure you two give to each other,* she warned herself. Still, the seed of hope she'd worked so hard to keep from germinating began to take root. *You can hope all you want to,* she told herself. *Just don't go letting your-self fall for the guy until you have some proof he cares for you.*

"I enjoy your company, too," she said, keeping her voice level. "And I know Josh would be happier if we all stayed together. Guess I might as well stick around."

Ryder nodded as if they'd just completed a busi-ness deal, then returned the conversation to the plans he had for the land.

Two Saturdays later Emily made her way toward the acreage Ryder had chosen for the stables and corral. Sam Marley had cut down the trees and carted them away within a couple of days after Ryder had con-tacted him. All of last weekend Ryder and Josh had worked on getting rid of the stumps. This weekend they were doing more of the same.

It was midafternoon. The day was clear and the weather had warmed. It was one of those days that felt more like early summer than early fall. After lunch Emily had busied herself in her garden. But the urge to see how Josh and Ryder were doing on their project was too strong. She'd saddled Lady Gray and ridden out.

"It's not really their progress that interests you," she mocked herself as she neared the cleared land. "You like to watch Ryder work." She scowled at this truth.

Just this morning she'd lain in bed watching him sleep. There are handsomer men in town, she'd reminded herself and tried to visualize one of them in bed beside her. The image had left her cold.

"As long as I don't start thinking of my life here as permanent, I won't get hurt," she assured herself as she rode toward the clearing. "I should just relax and enjoy myself and be prepared to leave the moment I know he's bored. That way my dignity will remain intact, my pride won't be injured, and I should be able to simply think of this part of my life as a fun time with no regrets." Satisfied she had her emotions in order, she urged her horse forward.

When she reached the clearing, she saw Ryder digging around the base of a particularly large stump. Josh was a short distance away on the tractor. A chain attached to the tractor had been wrapped securely around a smaller stump. Now Josh was preparing to use the tractor to pull that stump out.

Ryder saw Emily first. He'd paused to wipe the sweat from his face on the sleeve of his shirt. He raised his arm and waved.

Emily suddenly thought about the shower he'd be taking tonight and how much she'd like to climb in with him and wash him. She'd never done anything so overtly seductive. She'd always let him make the first move. Every time she'd considered initiating intimacy, she'd held back, afraid he might not be in the mood. It wouldn't hurt to be a little innovative, she decided as she waved back.

Not wanting Ryder to guess how intensely attracted she was to him, she turned her attention to Josh. He was looking over his shoulder at the stump, obviously checking the fastening of the chains. Then he gave the tractor some gas.

The stump didn't come up as easily as she'd thought it would. She heard the engine of the tractor rev. Josh was giving it more gas. In the next instant the tractor looked like a huge steel horse rearing on its hind legs as the chain tightened and the front wheels of the machine suddenly raised up into the air. Josh let out a yelp of surprise. Then he was falling. As he hit the ground the tractor began to fall over on top of him.

Emily's heart seemed to freeze in midbeat. She tried to shout, but a lump of panic was lodged in her throat.

Then suddenly the tractor was stopped, suspended in a tilted position, hovering over Josh.

"Pull Josh out of there!" Ryder yelled at her.

She glanced toward him to discover him simply standing watching the scene in front of him. Anger that he wasn't hurrying to help her son shot through her as she jumped from her saddle and raced to Josh's aid.

"Just got the wind knocked out of me," her son was saying, as she reached him. He was already worming his way out from under the shadow of the heavy machine.

"Give me your hands," she ordered, and willing every ounce of her strength into the effort, she pulled him totally free. Frantically her eyes scanned him for any signs of blood. There were none. "Are you hurt?" she demanded, attempting to determine if any internal damage had been done.

"Only my dignity got injured," he assured her, brushing himself off as he got to his feet.

Suddenly the ground beneath her shook. Dust and clods of dirt flew as the tractor slammed into the earth. Emily stood frozen, staring at it. She'd assumed its fall had been stopped above her son because it had landed against a stump. Now she realized that there had been nothing supporting the piece of equipment.

"Ryder!"

Josh's panicked cry caused her to spin around. Ryder was standing where she'd seen him before. His face was contorted with pain. Slowly he began to sink to his knees.

Josh raced toward him, with Emily following. Ryder, looking up from his kneeling position, focused his gaze on Josh. "Get me to the house. I need to rest," he said. Even in his weakened state, this came out sounding like an order.

Panic as great as what she'd felt when she'd seen the tractor falling on Josh filled Emily. She'd never imagined Ryder could look so weak. It was as if all his energy had been drained away.

"We have to get him to the truck," Josh said, his voice reflecting her panic.

Emily saw Ryder make a futile attempt to get to his feet. "You bring the truck here," she ordered Josh, dropping to her knees in front of Ryder.

"Right," Josh replied, already running toward the vehicle parked at the end of the rutted track left by the lumber trucks.

Emily turned her full attention to Ryder. "Looks like you could use some help," she said.

"Yeah," he admitted. "But wait until Josh brings the truck. I don't think I can stand very long."

Only a couple of minutes passed, but it seemed like forever before Josh pulled up beside them. When she tried to help Ryder to his feet, she couldn't. He was a dead weight. She had to get Josh to help her.

After they'd gotten Ryder into the passenger side of the cab, she climbed in with him to support him so that he wouldn't bang his head against the door as Josh drove them over the rough terrain. "Don't even stop at the house," she ordered her son. "Go straight to Dr. Prescott's office in town."

Ryder had been sitting, leaning heavily on her, his eyes closed. Now they opened and he looked at Josh. "Take me to the house and call your grandfather."

"You need to see a doctor," Emily protested, worried that he was going to pass out at any moment.

His hand closed around her wrist and, as weak as he was, his grip still felt like iron. "I know what I need, Emily," he growled. "Now do as I say."

She was about to tell him he was being stubborn and foolish. But as she started to speak, Josh interrupted.

"We'll do as you say," he promised Ryder.

Emily frowned impatiently at her son. "He needs a doctor."

"He knows what he needs," the boy replied without compromise.

Emily again started to protest, then stopped. In her mind's eye she was seeing the tractor poised above her son, held up by an invisible force long enough for Josh to escape injury.

"Ryder held the tractor without even touching it!" she breathed as the full impact of what had happened sank in.

"It'd be best if you didn't mention that to anyone except the Gerards," Josh warned, glancing toward her with a plea in his eyes.

Emily stared at her son. He didn't seem shocked or shaken, just worried.

"For Josh's sake, you'd be wise to heed his words," Ryder said.

Emily looked from man to boy. She wanted to demand an explanation of what was going on, but the anxious expression on her son's face as he drove let her know he needed to keep his attention on his driving. As for Ryder, a moan of discomfort escaped from him when the truck hit a particularly deep rut. This was neither the time nor the place for explanations, she decided.

At the house, she and Josh acted as human crutches, one under each of Ryder's arms, and managed to get him upstairs and into bed.

"I'll call Grandpa," Josh said.

"And I still think I should call the doctor," Emily muttered as she began removing Ryder's boots.

She felt him move and a hand closed around her arm. Startled, she turned to find him in a sitting position. *"No!"* he growled, then releasing her, he fell back against the pillows.

"You are the most stubborn man I've ever known," she fumed as she finished taking off his boots. When she heard no response, she turned to look at his face. His eyes were closed and he appeared to be asleep. It's more like he's in a coma, she thought a few minutes later. She'd stripped him down to his briefs and he didn't once give any indication that he even knew she was moving him around.

Suddenly he shivered and opened his eyes a crack. "I'm freezing," he complained groggily.

Quickly she pulled the covers over him. Straightening away from the bed, she looked down at him. The day was warm. He shouldn't have been cold. Her jaw firmed with resolve.

Going out into the hall, she nearly collided with Josh. "I'm going to call Dr. Prescott," she said curtly.

"Wait until Grandpa gets here," Josh pleaded. "He should be here any minute."

"I'm scared for Ryder, Josh," she said. "He—"

She was interrupted by the opening of the front door. Josh breathed a sigh of relief. "Grandpa's here," he said as if that would solve all their problems.

Emily turned to face Hobart Gerard as he hurried up the stairs and strode down the hall. "I'm going to call Dr. Prescott," she said with resolve.

"Just let me see Ryder first," he requested, coming to a stop in front of her. "I love my son. If he needs a doctor, I'll call Reid Prescott myself."

At least the man was talking as if he was open to the idea of seeking medical help, Emily thought. Still, she was afraid of waiting too long.

"I want your word you'll wait until I've seen Ryder for myself," Hobart demanded, regarding her sternly. "Both his future and your son's future could be at stake."

Emily was torn with indecision. There was an ominous quality in his voice that made her feel even more apprehensive. "I can't think straight," she said, her hands going up to her temples.

"Just give Grandpa a couple of minutes," Josh pleaded.

"All right," Emily agreed.

She hated herself for giving in. If anything happened to Ryder because of this delay, she'd never forgive herself. She paced up and down the hall anxiously. She could feel Josh's eyes on her. Coming to a halt in front of him, she said, "Would you please explain to me what happened out there with the tractor? How did Ryder stop it from falling?"

"It's something he can do—make things move with his mind," Josh replied, studying her worriedly. Hesitantly, he continued, "I can do it, too. Not as good as Ryder, but some. You won't start thinking of me as a freak, will you, Mom?"

Emily read the fear of rejection in his eyes. She held out her arms to him. "I will never think of you as anything other than my wonderful son," she said as he came into her arms. She hugged him to her. "I will always love you."

"I love you, too, Mom," he said in a voice filled with relief.

The door to Ryder's room opened. Releasing Josh, Emily turned to face Hobart.

"Ryder will be fine. He's simply exhausted and needs to rest," the man told her.

Hobart spoke with confidence, but Emily wasn't convinced. "It can't hurt to call the doctor," she argued. "We don't have to tell him how it happened. We can just say he was working too hard in the sun."

Hobart frowned impatiently. "The doctor won't be able to tell anything."

Emily told herself that Ryder's father knew the right thing to do. Still, the image of Ryder lying motionless and looking so drained haunted her. "Celina," Emily said as the burgundy-haired woman suddenly entered her mind.

Celina Prescott couldn't cure people, Emily knew. However, there were those who swore she could ease pain. Ryder's mother had been among them. Emily wasn't sure if this ability was real or if the people being touched were simply so certain it would work their own minds caused the pain to lessen. But what Emily was sure of was that Celina did have a knack for being able to tell if there was something wrong inside a person's body. Celina couldn't say what it was, but she could determine the location. And considering the circumstances, Emily thought Celina was the perfect choice to seek for medical advice regarding Ryder's condition.

"What about having Celina come out and check him?" she suggested.

Hobart shook his head. "That would raise a few eyebrows, which is just what Ryder doesn't want."

"We don't have to tell her what happened," Emily argued. "I could say that Ryder refused to allow me to call a doctor, but I couldn't stop worrying. And we could ask her not to say anything to anyone. Celina's not a gossip. She can keep a secret."

Hobart shook his head. "She always told Doc whenever anyone came to her for help. I know, because Doc came to see me after my wife asked Celina to help ease her pain. He wanted to make certain Edie continued to take her medicine as well. So, I think we can be real certain she's telling that doctor husband of hers who's calling on her."

"Most likely," Emily admitted. She'd seen the way Celina looked at Reid Prescott. It was the same way she herself had been looking at Ryder lately. Her jaw hardened. "Doctors take an oath. Their patients' illnesses are secret. Besides, what could either Dr. Prescott or Celina tell anyone? We'd tell them that Ryder collapsed in the field from exhaustion or heat stroke or something." Her gaze leveled on Hobart. "No one is going to ever guess the real reason."

Hobart took her hands in his. "Ryder will be all right. He just needs to rest," he said firmly.

Emily drew a shaky breath. His touch was comforting, but she was still uneasy.

"Grandpa knows what to do," Josh said. He'd been standing back, now he stepped up to stand beside his grandfather.

Emily's gaze searched the two of them. "If Ryder isn't better in twenty-four hours, I am going to call Celina," she stated with resolve.

"If he's not better in twenty-four hours, I'll call her myself," Hobart promised.

"I'm going to go sit with him," she said. "And if he begins to look worse, I'm calling her immediately."

Hobart gave her an encouraging smile. "That's a good idea. You go sit with him. He should have someone there in case he needs anything."

Josh fell into step beside her. "I'll come, too."

Abruptly Emily came to a halt. "Lady Gray!" The name blurted out as she remembered the horse she'd been riding. "I left her in the clearing."

"No need to worry," Hobart assured her. "I saw her down by the corral when I drove up. She always finds her way home." His gaze shifted to Josh. "But she should be unsaddled and maybe given a good brushing."

Concern for the mare showed on Josh's face. Turning to his mother, he said, "I'll be back in a little while," then hurried off to take care of the animal.

As Emily went into the bedroom and sat in the chair by the window, she was glad for a few minutes alone with Ryder. She drew a shaky breath. She felt as anxious for his safety as she would have if Josh had been the one lying there.

The tractor incident played through her mind. Then she recalled her first night and day in this house. There had been the glass of water she'd almost spilled and the bowl of batter that had stopped just short of falling off the counter. He'd stopped those accidents from happening—she was certain of it. A smile suddenly tilted one corner of her mouth. That door closing the first morning they'd made love hadn't been a breeze, either, she guessed.

Another memory turned her smile into a thoughtful frown. Ryder had mentioned watching her riding her father's horse when she'd been a young girl. She'd ridden bareback with only the horse's mane to hold on to. During those moments of stolen freedom, there had been several times when she'd thought she was going to fall. The time she'd jumped the horse over that gully, she'd been sure she was going to lose her balance and her grip. But almost as if gentle hands had been holding her, she'd remained on the horse's back. Now, it occurred to her that Ryder had been the reason she'd been saved from injury.

This ability he had should cause her to be afraid of him. It certainly wasn't normal. But she wasn't afraid or even a little apprehensive. *What I am is desperately worried about him and deeply in love with him,* she admitted.

A knock on the door interrupted her thoughts. Before she could rise to answer it, Justin Gerard entered.

Like Ryder's, Justin's eyes were a deep brown, and while the rest of him showed signs of his eighty years, those eyes were as sharp as a youngster's. "I thought you and I should have a talk," he said. "I suppose you have a few questions, and it's time you had the answers."

Chapter Ten

"I would like a few answers," Emily said as the elderly man reached the companion chair to hers.

Justin moved his chair until it directly faced hers. "And you shall have them," he promised, seating himself.

She met his gaze. "When my great-grandfather, Thaddeus Sayer, claimed he saw your father, Zachariah Gerard move that tree without touching it, he was telling the truth, wasn't he?" she said.

"He was telling the truth," Justin admitted. "And for your son's sake, I hope you'll keep what you know about us a secret."

Emily suddenly found herself picturing Beatrice setting the table by simply standing in the center of the kitchen and moving the dishes out of the cabinets with her thoughts. "Do all of you have this ability?"

Justin shook his head. "No. Ryder is the only one of his siblings to have it, and neither Hobart nor I have the talent. My brother has some small ability." He frowned thoughtfully. "I used to think Beatrice might have a knack for it. She's always seemed to me to stand apart, but I guess that's just that strong streak of independence in her. Anyway, the talent has never manifested itself in her." He glanced toward the bed where Ryder lay. "Even when a person does have the talent, it's rarely as strong as my grandson's. Holding that tractor is something I don't think even Zachariah could have done."

The fear that the Gerards weren't totally human filled Emily. "Who are you? *What* are you?" she demanded.

Reaching over, Justin gave her hand a reassuring squeeze. "We're human just like you," he said. Releasing her hand, he continued quietly, "Our ancestors were druids, singled out for the priesthood because of their unique ability. Perhaps there was even some selective breeding—that we'll never know. What I do know is that the druids were a people who believed in drawing their strength from within themselves and from nature—the air, the trees, the water. I suppose you could say they had a holistic approach to life."

"And all of the members of the priesthood had Ryder's ability?" Emily asked, suddenly wondering if the druids really were responsible for Stonehenge. Or maybe Merlin, the sorcerer from the Arthurian legends, had been an especially powerful druid.

"No." Justin shook his head, giving emphasis to this denial. "Others were seers, prophets—fortune-tellers, if you will. Their abilities were varied, encompassing all of what is today labeled psychic powers. Some, supposedly, even had a talent for healing. Because of these unique abilities, they were both feared and respected by their own people. They became the law-givers and the arbitrators in disputes. Then outsiders came, intent on taking the druids' land and ruling them. These conquerors were powerful and many. The druids fought fiercely, but in the end were defeated. The victors, fearful of the talents of the priesthood, attempted to annihilate all druids. Those who managed to escape fled and hid their real identities. Through the centuries, they assimilated into other cultures.''

Again he leaned toward her and took her hand. ''People fear what they don't understand. My family has learned that it is best to keep our talent a secret.''

The history of Smytheshire suddenly played through Emily's mind. The town wasn't that old. Just before the turn of the century, Angus Smythe had come to this valley and bought up several adjoining farms. He'd cleared an area for the town and begun building homes, along with structures that now housed the various businesses. Soon after, people began to arrive and Smytheshire had been born.

She could still remember hearing her grandfather complain about all the new people coming into the area. He'd been afraid their valley would get overpopulated. But after the first couple of years, the growth had slowed to close to a standstill. The Smythes hadn't encouraged any large industry to move into the area. There were a couple of cottage industries in town. Morgan Norwood made beautiful ce-

ramic bowls, dishes and other utensils, which he sold
to stores in large cities, and Janis Troy made jewelry.
But Morgan only employed a couple of people and
Janis had a single employee. Farming and some tour-
ism were the main sources of income. Thus, the town
had remained small—a comfortable, quaint, peaceful
community nestled in the Massachusetts countryside.

But the Sayers had continued to act as if their land
had been invaded by strangers. Emily knew that this
was partially because a Sayer had originally owned a
great deal of the land on which Smytheshire was built.
Her grandfather and her great-grandfather were still
furious with their relative for selling out. They felt the
land should have stayed in the family. But the cousin
who had sold out had never gotten along with the rest
of the family, and Angus had offered double the market value. As for Emily's father, even though he'd
married the daughter of one of the newly arrived
families, he also considered the majority of the residents of Smytheshire interlopers.

Suddenly, a thought entered Emily's mind and she
studied Justin narrowly. "Celina isn't exactly a healer
but she does have a certain talent for diagnosing. Old
Mrs. Elberly swears her crystals sing to her. And I've
heard that Mary Beth Logan is particularly good at
palm readings." She looked hard into the old man's
eyes. "Are all of you who came here to Smytheshire
of druid ancestry?"

Justin grinned. "You're a bright girl," he said.
"The answer to your question is that some are and
some aren't." He held up a hand. "Don't ask me who
is and who isn't, because I can't tell you. I could make
a good guess in some cases, but there isn't any way of

really telling unless you see the talent being used." His expression became thoughtful. "Being here as long as I have, it's my feeling that a lot of those who have druid ancestry don't know about it. It's for sure that those who do know aren't talking about it."

Emily wasn't convinced. "If that's the case, then how did so many of you end up in the same place?" An uneasiness spread through her. "Do you have some sort of homing sense that draws all of you together?"

Justin smiled warmly. "No, girl," he said with a laugh. "It was Angus Smythe who brought us together." He paused and his smile faded. "There were a couple of other times through the centuries that Angus's ancestors tried to pull druid descendants together. The communities failed. This time it seems Angus decided to get us together but not let us know he was doing it or why."

"I'm very confused now," Emily confessed.

"Centuries ago when we all fled in every direction, Angus's ancestors must have kept track of as many of us as they could. That would explain how they were able to find us. My guess is they've kept written records. As far as I know, they're the only ones who did. Everything I've ever learned was passed down verbally through my family. Each time a community decided that for their safety they must again disperse, a pact to forget and not repeat any of the names was made among the members. Then everyone would go their own way and seek out new existences. The only name my family didn't erase from memory was the Smythe name. 'There's good Smythes and there's bad

Smythes,' my great-grandfather used to say. 'Best be cautious around all of them.'

"But your family came here," Emily pointed out, finding herself fascinated by the old man's revelations.

"One day near the turn of the century, Zachariah's daddy, Innis Gerard, received a letter from a lawyer saying some long-lost relative had died and left us this big piece of acreage in Massachusetts. When Innis came out here to inspect the land and discovered the nearest town was named Smytheshire and had been founded by an Angus Smythe, he was suspicious. He made a point of meeting Angus. As if discussing an interest in history, Innis mentioned the druids. He saw a light flicker in Angus's eyes. As the evening progressed, Angus admitted that he was seeking to bring our people back together. But he also swore he had no intention of attempting to resurrect the past. He made it clear that he intended Smytheshire to be a normal, conservative, quiet, comfortable small town just like any other in the country. And there would be those who weren't of our heritage living here. This was necessary, because he needed various professional people to create a viable community. He swore that he merely wanted to create a safe place for those of our ilk to live. He did sort of probe around trying to find out if any of our family possessed any of the talents, but Innis played dumb on that point."

Justin's gaze narrowed on her. "Zachariah was going on ten then and already showing signs of having the talent. It occurred to his daddy that if they were living among others with talents, Zachariah would be safer."

Emily nodded her understanding. Exposure of the type of talent the Gerards possessed could be dangerous. If Thaddeus Sayer had had his way, Zachariah would have been tarred and feathered, or worse.

Justin looked relieved. "Anyway, Zachariah's father decided to move here. But he vowed he'd fight any attempt to resurrect the pagan culture of our ancestors. He knew there were those who might believe that a return to ancient customs and practices could cause them to gain the powers their ancestors had possessed. But Innis and his family knew that no silly superstitious practices could give anyone any of the talents. Either a person is born with one, or they're not. If not then they're never going to have one. There's no two ways about it. Guess the others who know about their heritage, if there are any, feel the same. Soon after the town really began to take shape, Angus started talking about starting up a study group centering on ancient cultures. No one showed any interest, but Innis was worried. He went to see Angus and told him he'd leave if Angus continued with this or any other ploy. Angus immediately dropped the idea and after that abided by his word to allow Smytheshire to remain an ordinary rural American community."

"My son has the Gerard talent," Emily said, bringing the subject back to the present.

Justin nodded. "Yes. We've been keeping an eye on the boy since his birth. If he had the talent, we knew we had to train him. Even more, he would need to understand that there was nothing wrong with him, that what was happening was natural for him."

"Yes," Emily agreed quietly, recalling Josh's withdrawal and uneasiness during the preceding winter and spring. More importantly, she remembered her son's concern that she would think he was a freak.

"In some cases, like with Zachariah and Ryder, the talent becomes obvious at an early age," Justin continued. "In others, usually when the talent is less strong, it won't begin to manifest itself until the person is into his teens. For someone who doesn't expect it, that discovery can be confusing and frightening. Last year when Josh began to be a problem, we suspected he was discovering his gift. Then last spring Ryder spotted him down by the river causing branches to go against the current."

"And so Ryder decided it was time to step into Josh's life and help him," Emily finished.

"Something like that," Justin replied. He rose slowly, then looking down at her, added, "Because I know how much you love your son, I've told you everything. I hope you'll consider the consequences for Josh if you should reveal what you now know."

Emily stood and offered him her hand. "You have my word. I'll keep your secret."

Accepting her handshake as her bond, he smiled approvingly. "You're a good woman, Emily." Then he released her, and left the room.

Alone with Ryder, Emily wished he, too, thought of her as a good woman—good enough to fall in love with. When he was better, she would court him, she decided. After all, he'd asked her to stay. That meant he must have enjoyed her company a great deal. Her attempt to get him to release his heart to her might prove futile, but he was worth the effort.

Sitting back in her chair, she watched the man on the bed. "You get well fast, Ryder Gerard," she said in hushed tones, "because I have plans for us."

A light knock on the door woke Emily. A sharp pain shot through her neck as she straightened in the chair. The hands of the clock on the bedside table were pointing to near midnight. She'd been sitting in that chair so long it was beginning to feel like a part of her. She'd even eaten dinner here in Ryder's room. Josh had come up soon after that and wanted to keep the vigil with her for the entire night, but she'd sent him to bed a couple of hours ago.

Beatrice had come up soon after Josh had left and offered to stay with Ryder, but Emily had insisted on remaining. If he did show any signs of getting worse she wanted to be there. But he actually seemed to be sleeping more and more peacefully as time went on. The strength had returned to his face and his breathing was deeper.

Before Emily could respond to the knock on the door, Hobart Gerard entered. "Just thought I'd come in and check for myself," he said, striding over to the bed and looking down at his son. Relief showed on his face. "He looks much better," he announced with approval. He seated himself in the chair his father had occupied earlier. "Beatrice has a turkey in the oven and some bread rising. When Ryder wakes he's going to be starved," he informed her. "He'll eat and then sleep some more. Could be three or four days or more before he's totally fit again. A tractor is one heck of a load to hold."

Emily frowned thoughtfully as she glanced at the man lying on the bed. "The funny thing is I feel like I should still be having a hard time believing he did it. But I'm not."

Hobart smiled. "I was worried about this marriage between him and you. I knew it was necessary for Josh's sake, but I didn't want Ryder sacrificing his life to make amends for his brother's behavior." A sadness descended over Hobart's features. "But then, Ryder's always felt overly responsible where Hallam was concerned."

The phrase "sacrificing his life" and "overly responsible" caused an uneasiness to spread through Emily.

Hobart leaned forward and took her hand in his. "I want to apologize for what Hallam did to you. In a way we were all responsible for what happened." Releasing her, the sadness returned to his face. "Not having the talent never bothered me. To tell the truth, it made my life a lot easier. Having the talent is like having a third arm you have to keep hidden and never use when anyone can see you. Hallam didn't inherit the talent either, but he didn't see it my way. He wanted the ability so badly, he even made himself sick a few times. He'd stare at an object trying to move it until he had a headache so bad he'd throw up."

Hobart shook his head. "I tried to explain to him that the talent wasn't a blessing. And Ryder didn't flaunt his ability. In fact, he once told Hallam that if he could, he'd give his gift to his brother. But it doesn't work that way. Hallam got more frustrated and bitter. Ryder felt guilty because he had the talent and didn't want it, and Hallam wanted it so desperately."

"So Ryder spent his time trying to undo any damage Hallam did," Emily finished.

"Yes. After you got pregnant, Ryder appointed himself your guardian angel. He was only eighteen at the time, but he was determined to see that you and the child were safe." Hobart breathed a sigh of relief. "I'm glad things have worked out so well. I know Ryder's been worried about how you would accept the knowledge of his and Josh's ability. Now he'll be able to put his mind at ease."

As Hobart left and Emily was again alone with Ryder, she fought to hold back the tears that flooded her eyes. Now she understood. Ryder had never married, never allowed himself to fall in love, because he felt responsible for her and Josh. He didn't love her, and one day he would resent her. Just the thought of his rejection brought a sharp jab of pain. Even more importantly, he deserved to have his own life. Emily knew what she had to do. She had to set him free.

Ryder awoke late the following afternoon. Like Hobart had predicted, he ate ravenously, then slept again.

Satisfied he was on the road to recovery, Beatrice and Hobart left him in Emily's care. That night she sat in Ryder's room again. Ever since deciding she'd have to free him, she'd held a running debate with herself. A part of her wanted to remain in his bed, sharing his company until the adoption was completed. But another part was afraid to continue the intimacy. The thought of leaving him hurt already. If she went back to his bed, when the adoption was finished and the time came for her to let him go, that hurt would only be multiplied.

In the early hours of the morning, he awoke again. When he'd awoken before, he'd only had the strength to eat and go back to sleep. He'd barely spoken a word. She expected the same this time, but as she entered the room with the tray of food, she discovered him sitting at the table.

"Shouldn't you be in bed?" she asked, concerned by the tired lines still etched into his face.

"I want to take a shower after I eat, then I'll sleep again." He studied her as she set the food in front of him. "How's Josh?"

"He's fine," she assured him.

"I've seen you sleeping in that chair." He nodded toward the chair she'd occupied so much of the past couple of days. "You would have been more comfortable in the bed."

"I didn't want to disturb your rest." She shifted her gaze away from him as she spoke so he wouldn't see the flash of pain in her eyes.

"I guess my dad explained everything to you."

Hearing the uneasiness in his voice, she looked at him. "Actually it was your grandfather who told me the whole story."

"You don't have to be afraid of me or Josh," he growled.

She frowned impatiently. "I'm most certainly not afraid of my son and I'm not afraid of you, either."

A coolness descended over his features. "But you're not comfortable around me now, are you?"

"No." She knew he thought her discomfort was

because of his talent. And pride wouldn't allow her to tell him differently. Besides, if he knew the truth, he'd be the one feeling uncomfortable around her.

He regarded her dryly. "Guess you won't be coming back to my bed at all."

"Guess not."

"I never really expected things to work out between me and you," he said with a note of finality.

He was certainly taking their break well, she thought wryly. *He's probably relieved,* she added. As for herself, she'd known this moment would be difficult. What she hadn't expected was the extent of the pain. Her stomach had knotted into a ball so tight she could barely breathe. "You'd better eat and rest some more," she instructed, heading for the door. She had to get out of there before she made a fool of herself by crying or saying something stupid.

A few minutes later she heard the water running in his bathroom. Hot tears burned at the back of her eyes as she recalled her plan to climb into the shower with him the next time he bathed. *At least I discovered the truth about his feelings for me before I let him know how deeply I've learned to care for him,* she thought. That would have placed both of them in an embarrassing situation.

Entering his room while he was still in the shower, she noted that he'd again eaten all the food she'd brought. She quickly straightened the bed. Then retrieving the tray, she left. She knew it was cowardly not to wait in the room until she knew he was safely back in bed, but again she was afraid she might do or say something that would expose her true feelings and embarrass him.

Out in the hall, she stood silently listening as he turned off the shower and then moved around the bedroom. Not until she heard the bed creak and knew he was again lying down, did she take the tray to the kitchen.

Giving him time to go back to sleep, she busied herself downstairs for the next half an hour. To her relief he was sleeping soundly when she returned to his room. For a long moment she stood watching him. A hurt like none she'd ever felt enveloped her. Jerking her gaze away, she began gathering her things and removing them from the bedroom.

Chapter Eleven

"**I** want to know why you've moved out of Ryder's room."

Emily turned to see Josh standing in the doorway of the kitchen. It was five days since the accident with the tractor. Ryder had returned to his daily routine, and she'd seen Josh drive off to school a little while ago. But obviously he'd come back.

"At first I thought you were sleeping in your old room so he could rest better. I figured you would move back as soon as he was well. But you haven't," Josh continued. Accusation mingled in his voice with anxiety. "Did you lie to me when you said the talent didn't bother you?"

"No, that wasn't a lie," she assured him. "But knowing about it has helped me understand a few things about Ryder. He's been real good to us through the years. He's sacrificed having a life of his own so he could watch over us." Approaching her son, she laid her hands on his shoulders. "Although Ryder has been very good to me, he doesn't really want to be married to me. He deserves to have a life free from any obligations he feels to us. Even more, he deserves to have a wife he truly wants. We both owe him a lot. I want him to be happy and I know you do, too."

"I thought the two of you were getting along real well," Josh said, clearly not wanting to give up the hope that his mother and Ryder would stay married.

"Life doesn't always work out the way you want it to," Ryder's voice sounded from behind Emily. Swinging around, she saw him standing in the doorway leading to the back porch. "You're practically an adult now, Josh," he added curtly. "Your mother has devoted her life to raising you. It's time for her to go her own way."

"You're right," Josh replied. His gaze shifted from Ryder to his mother, then back to Ryder. "You're both right." He didn't look happy, Emily thought, but he did look resigned to the fact that this marriage was not going to last.

"You better be getting to school. You're going to be late as it is," Ryder ordered.

Josh nodded. Turning to his mother, he said solemnly, "You know what's best." Then he gave her a hug and left.

"I saw the boy come back." Ryder stepped into the room just far enough to let the screened door close behind him. "I knew he'd been watching us the past few days. I figured he'd come back to confront you."

"I should have spoken to him sooner," Emily replied. Ryder was watching her with that cool distant expression he'd used so often in the past. Suddenly she felt exhausted. She called herself a fool. She'd been missing Ryder so horribly she hadn't slept well these past nights. The unexpected sound of water running in the sink caused her to jerk around. She saw the cabinet door to the right open and a glass float out. The glass positioned itself under the running water. When it was three-quarters full, it moved to the counter. Next the water was turned off. Then the glass began to move across the room until it reached Ryder. She saw the challenge in his eyes. He didn't believe she wasn't afraid of him. He expected her to run screaming from the room. She scowled at him.

"If you wanted a drink, all you had to do was ask," she said.

Ryder studied her narrowly as he sat the glass down undrunk. "I did that once in front of my mother and saw fear in her eyes. But my being able to think things to move really doesn't bother you, does it?"

"I told you it didn't," she snapped.

"Then I don't understand why you're avoiding me," he growled.

"For the reasons I gave Josh," she said. "I know you only married me out of duty. Now that I know the truth, there's no reason for you to feel beholden to me any longer. What Hallam did was *his* sin, not yours. You shouldn't have to pay for it for the rest of your life."

His expression turned grim. "You're wrong. What happened to you was at least partially my fault. Hallam coveted everything that was mine or everything he thought I wanted. He saw me looking at you, and that

was why he went after you." Abruptly Ryder turned
and stalked out of the kitchen.

Emily stood staring at the empty doorway. Questions flooded her mind. Fear that his answers wouldn't
be what she wanted to hear held her immobile. A person has to take a chance once in a while, she reminded herself, and raced out the back door after him.

Reaching him, she caught his arm. Mistake! her
mind screamed as the heat traveled through her and all
she wanted was to be held by him. He had to give her
the right answers before she could give in to that urge.
"Ryder, wait," she demanded, hurriedly releasing him
as he stopped and looked down at her.

Her quick release was not lost on him. "You don't
have to be afraid to touch me," he snarled.

"Maybe I do," she returned, then wished she'd held
her tongue as he glared at her and started walking
away again.

"Ryder, stop!" she called, afraid to touch him
again. If she did, she might blurt out all her feelings
and embarrass herself and him.

Without even a backward glance, he kept walking.

She jogged after him. "You're not being fair," she
accused in frustration. "I can't close doors or move
objects in front of you to stop you."

That brought him to a halt. Turning, he faced her
coldly. "What do you want?"

The coldness in his eyes threatened her nerve, but
she forced herself to continue. "I want to know what
you meant when you said Hallam saw you looking at
me. I want to know how you were looking at me."

"Like I wanted to have you for dessert," he replied
icily.

A burst of joy shot through her. It was quickly followed by a rebirth of her ingrained caution. Afraid to freely allow herself to believe the implication in this admission, she said tersely, "In all the years we were growing up, I never saw you look at me with anything but disinterest."

"You never looked at me with anything but distaste," he returned.

"You were always glaring at me," she shot back.

Ryder's gaze turned even colder. "You were a Sayer. I couldn't get you off my mind, but I couldn't trust you. I figured if you ever learned about my talent, you'd be horrified. You'd tell the world and have me and my family labeled as freaks."

Her shoulders squared as the insult reddened her cheeks. But as she was about to give him a piece of her mind, the words caught in her throat. Instead, she admitted, "I suppose I can understand how you could feel that way."

"When Hallam told me you were pregnant with his child, I felt as if I'd been punched in the stomach. I know now he was lying when he said you'd seduced him. At the time, however, I was jealous as hell. But I was still willing to marry you. I figured getting you into my bed was the only way I was going to get you out of my system. But you refused."

The image of him standing in the entrance of her cave all those years ago filled Emily's mind while his words caused a hollowness inside her. "You're just talking about lust," she said, the hope that had brought her racing after him dying.

"If what I feel for you is merely lust, it's one hell of a strong case," he growled. "I married you just to get you under my roof. I could have handled Josh in other ways. He's a reasonable boy, and good-natured. I could have befriended him as his uncle. As for his being a Gerard, my family could have simply claimed him. And that probably would have been for the best. My brother put you through hell. When you told me what he'd done, I almost backed out on the marriage. But I was selfish. I knew I'd never have any peace if I walked away again."

Emily frowned in confusion. "But you made it clear you never intended to consummate our marriage."

He drew a harsh breath. "All these years you've plagued me. I figured if I could spend some time with you, just day-to-day living, having you around on a continuous basis would get you out of my system. But it didn't work that way. I wanted you even more."

Emily studied him silently. What he was talking about could still be nothing more than lust.

He issued a short self-mocking laugh. "When you did come to my bed, I was sure that would end my craving for you. Instead, I found myself wanting to ask you have my children and stay with me forever." Cynicism etched itself into his features. "But I was sure you wouldn't be able to accept living with me when you learned about my secret. My own mother had a difficult time dealing with the gift. Still, I couldn't stop myself from asking you to stay."

His jaw tensed. "Obviously I was wrong. My talent doesn't bother you. You just aren't interested in being tied to me." Again he started to walk away.

He still hadn't actually said he loved her, but he'd made it clear he wanted her to stay and was very attracted to her. *Take a chance!* she ordered herself. "I would very much like to have your children," she said.

Ryder came to an abrupt halt.

"I thought you'd be glad to get rid of me," she said to his back. "I was rejected once by everyone I thought loved me and who I loved. I couldn't bear to go through that again. I thought you only made the offer for me to stay out of a sense of duty. I was sure one day you'd regret it and turn against me."

He turned and strode toward her. "I will never regret keeping you, Emily," he swore. Reaching her, he drew her into his embrace. "I love you," he said gruffly. "Through the years, I've tried denying it, but I've always loved you."

Joy filled her. "I love you," she admitted.

He grinned with relief and satisfaction. "Seems to me I could use another day in bed," he said, leaning down and nibbling on her ear.

Shivers of delight flowed through her. She'd never believed she could be this happy. "An extra day of bed rest is always good," she replied.

"'Rest' wasn't exactly what I had in mind," he growled against her lips.

"I'm very glad to hear that," she admitted, thinking that nothing could feel so wonderful as being in his arms.

"Emily."

Emily had been lying quietly on her back with her eyes closed, feeling totally contented and at peace with the world. Opening her eyes, she discovered Ryder propped on an elbow watching her.

The morning's lovemaking had been more exciting and fulfilling than any before because she'd known his heart was in it. But now there was a guardedness in his eyes. She had a sudden fear that he hadn't been honest with her. "Is something wrong?" she asked.

"No, not wrong," he replied.

She saw the indecision on his face and tensed. "Clearly something is bothering you. Have you suddenly discovered that what you thought was love was merely lust and you're now bored with me?" she demanded, the words cutting into her like knives.

"No, definitely not." Leaning down, he kissed her. "I will never be bored with you."

His kiss and the sincerity in his voice healed her hurt, but still she was uneasy. "Would you please tell me what's bothering you?" she coaxed.

"It's something that's been nagging at the back of my mind ever since our wedding day." The indecision again was strong on his face. "You might not like hearing it."

The seriousness in his eyes was making her nervous. "Well, it's obvious it's something we need to talk about. Do I have some little habit that irritates you?"

Smiling as if this was an absurd notion, he kissed the tip of her nose. "I love your little habits, especially the one where you stretch when you're waking up. It makes me think of a cat on a lazy summer afternoon."

"Ryder!" she snapped. "Will you please tell me what the problem is?"

His smile disappeared and he regarded her soberly. "I think you're an enhancer."

She stared at him in confusion. "An enhancer? What's an enhancer?"

"You increase my power," he replied. "That first night when you almost knocked the glass of water over... When I started to stop it, I almost spilled it in the other direction. I figured maybe that was just nerves. Having you here in this house was making me tense." Grinning, he kissed her lightly. Then his expression became serious once again. "But the next morning I noticed that I had to curb the energy I used to stop the bowl of batter from going off the table. The tractor was the real test. I don't think I could have held it above Josh if you hadn't been there. In the past, I've experimented with my ability to measure just how strong it is. I figure I could have slowed the tractor's fall so that Josh might have had time to escape. Or I could have caused it to fall more lightly. But I couldn't have, on my own, held it suspended the way I did for the length of time I did."

Emily regarded him thoughtfully. "My grandparents on my mother's side were one of the families who moved to Smytheshire from the outside. They came from Oregon. And they never claimed any close relatives." Her eyes gleamed. "I suppose they could have been one of those families with druid heritage."

"My guess is they were," Ryder replied, relief evident on his face. "I'm glad you don't mind."

Emily grinned mischievously. "I like the idea of being able to enhance your power."

Laughing, Ryder pulled her into his arms.

"I wonder if my presence would enhance other people's powers," she mused as he nibbled her ear.

Lifting his head away from her, he regarded her with mock sternness. "Right now, I'd appreciate it if you'd concentrate on me."

"That," she said with a gentle laugh, "would be my pleasure." And as his lips found hers, she forgot about everything but the warmth of his love.

*   *   *   *   *

Silhouette Books
is proud to present
our best authors,
their best books...
and the best in
your reading pleasure!

Throughout 1993, look for exciting
books by these top names in
contemporary romance:

DIANA PALMER—
Fire and Ice in June

ELIZABETH LOWELL—
Fever in July

CATHERINE COULTER—
Afterglow in August

LINDA HOWARD—
Come Lie With Me in September

When it comes to passion,
we wrote the book.

BOBT2

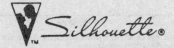

Take 4 bestselling love stories FREE

Plus get a FREE surprise gift!

Special Limited-time Offer

Mail to Silhouette Reader Service®

P.O. Box 609
Fort Erie, Ontario
L2A 5X3

YES! Please send me 4 free Silhouette Romance® novels and my free surprise gift. Then send me 6 brand-new novels every month, which I will receive months before they appear in bookstores. Bill me at the low price of $2.25 each plus 25¢ delivery and GST*. That's the complete price and—compared to the cover prices of $2.75 each—quite a bargain! I understand that accepting the books and gift places me under no obligation ever to buy any books. I can always return a shipment and cancel at any time. Even if I never buy another book from Silhouette, the 4 free books and the surprise gift are mine to keep forever.

315 BPA AJJF

Name	(PLEASE PRINT)	
Address	Apt. No.	
City	Province	Postal Code

THIS SIDE OF HEAVEN

The miracle of love is waiting to be discovered in Duncan, Oklahoma! Arlene James takes you there in her new trilogy, THIS SIDE OF HEAVEN.

Begin your visit to Duncan with an emotional story of love's healing strength:

The Perfect Wedding

Rod Corley was planning a wedding that he hoped would clear his family's scandalous reputation. Luckily for Layne Harrington, Rod wasn't the groom. But would Layne's love be enough to help Rod forget the past?

Available in September,
only from

Silhouette
R O M A N C E™

Silhouette Books has done it again!

Opening night in October has never been as exciting! Come watch as the curtain rises and romance flourishes when the stars of tomorrow make their debuts today!

Revel in Jodi O'Donnell's STILL SWEET ON HIM—
Silhouette Romance #969
...as Callie Farrell's renovation of the family homestead leads her straight into the arms of teenage crush Drew Barnett!

Tingle with Carol Devine's BEAUTY AND THE BEASTMASTER—
Silhouette Desire #816
...as legal eagle Amanda Tarkington is carried off by wrestler Bram Masterson!

Thrill to Elyn Day's A BED OF ROSES—
Silhouette Special Edition #846
...as Dana Whitaker's body and soul are healed by sexy physical therapist Michael Gordon!

Believe when Kylie Brant's McLAIN'S LAW—
Silhouette Intimate Moments #528
...takes you into detective Connor McLain's life as he falls for psychic—and suspect—Michele Easton!

Catch the classics of tomorrow—*premiering* today—
only from ❤ *Silhouette*

Dear Reader,

We hope you've enjoyed reading Ryder and Emily's story and are looking
forward to the upcoming books that take place in Smytheshire. We value
your opinions and invite you to write to us, telling us what you like about
A Wedding For Emily and the Smytheshire, Massachusetts series. Did you
enjoy reading about Ryder's telekinetic powers (i.e., his ability to move
objects with his thoughts)? Did you enjoy reading the explanation for
Ryder's powers, which concerned the Druid ancestry in Smytheshire? Why
or why not? What did you enjoy most about the story and why? What are
your favorite types of romance stories (e.g., plots: marriage of convenience,
stories with Western settings, business settings; characters: older or
younger hero/heroine, rich hero, innocent heroine, etc.)? Along with your
letter, please answer the following questionnaire, and mail both to:

Customer Opinion Center
P.O. Box 1387
Buffalo, NY 14240-9990

Your comments are important to us. Thank you for sharing them with us.

Anne Canadeo
Silhouette Books

---

1. **How likely are you to purchase more books in the Smytheshire series?**
   ☐ Definitely will purchase   ☐ Probably will not purchase
   ☐ Probably will purchase   ☐ Definitely will not purchase

2. **Which statement best describes how often you read Silhouette Romance books?**
   ☐ At least 1 per month   ☐ At least 1 per year
   ☐ At least 1 every other month ☐ This is my first time

3. **Of all the romance books you have read in the past year, what three books were your favorites?** _____
   _____

4. **Where do you usually buy romance paperbacks?**
   ☐ Supermarket   ☐ Discount Store   ☐ Mail Subscription   ☐ Other
   ☐ Drugstore   ☐ Used Bookstore   ☐ Bookstore

5. **Please indicate your age range:**
   ☐ under 18   ☐ 25 to 34   ☐ 50 to 64
   ☐ 18 to 24   ☐ 35 to 49   ☐ 65 or older

QSR03